j
c.2

Madison, Winifred
    Becky's horse.   Four Winds Press
[1975]
    152 p.

I. Title

BECKY'S HORSE

By the same author

Maria Luisa
Max's Wonderful Delicatessen
Growing Up in a Hurry
Bird on the Wing

BECKY'S HORSE

by Winifred Madison

j
c. 2

Four Winds Press
New York

Library of Congress Cataloging in Publication Data

Madison, Winifred.
   Becky's horse.

   SUMMARY: Becky must decide whether to keep the
horse she won or take the prize money to help an Austrian
cousin orphaned during the invasion of Hitler's troops.

   1. Title.
PZ7.M2652Be   [Fic]   74–26717
ISBN 0–590–07361–3

Published by Four Winds Press
A Division of Scholastic Magazines, Inc., New York, N.Y.
Copyright © 1975 by Winifred Madison

For Ethel

1
Becky Takes a Ride

Becky was daydreaming. The day, a Friday, was gentle and sunlit, an unexpected jewel among the cold gray days of February. Miss Robertson, however, seemed to find it less than perfect. Its effect on the seventh grade classroom was disastrous.

"All right, class. Let's pay attention. Who can tell me what a verb is. Does anyone know? Anyone at all?" Miss Robertson pleaded.

Never had there been such squirming, wiggling, and jumping up and down in her classroom. Even the students who usually sat with hands folded all through the class were throwing paper airplanes and begging to go to the water fountain every few seconds. The shuffling of restless feet promised that when the bell rang, everyone would flee from the classroom.

Although Becky was sitting quietly, Miss Robertson had the feeling that her mind was elsewhere. She was right. Becky's thoughts wandered here and there, to her little sister, Dori, whose best friend had moved away that very morning. Poor Dori, how sad she was. "I'll play with her after school," Becky promised, even though Dori was only six.

"Can't anyone tell me what a verb is?" Miss Robertson begged. Nobody volunteered, so she answered the question herself.

"Verbs are words that *go!*"

"And I wish I could go with them," Becky groaned to herself. She was hungry, she decided, starving in fact, although she had had lunch only a short while ago. Tonight was Sabbath and dinner would be particularly good because Papa was working again. And Mama had probably invited some aunt or cousin to join them. If only they didn't talk about how awful everything was in Europe, she wouldn't mind so much.

"But I won't last till tonight," she thought, and glanced across the room to catch the eye of Lisa Kline so she could mouth out the message, "Let's get some ice cream after school!" but Lisa was passing notes to Robbie and tittering, so Becky gave up.

For the tenth time that hour, Becky looked up at the clock. The big hand pointed to the ten and the little hand was close to the two. Hadn't it been exactly like that at least five minutes ago when Becky looked up at the clock? A discovery, the clock had stopped! She would count five and then thrust her arm into the air with the news.

"Miss Robertson, the clock has stopped."

There would be a moment of stunned silence, then applause. Miss Robertson would look at her watch and find it was three thirty, time to go home!

But it wasn't to be. A splintery click moved the long hand of the clock ahead one stingy minute.

"Oh, no," Becky groaned. "Almost two hours more."

"Come, class, let's name some verbs. Surely you can think of a few on a nice day like this," Miss Robertson begged. Poor Miss Robertson!

Becky thought of verbs in silence. "Gallop, trot, canter, ride."

It was then that the shining chestnut mare walked through the door. Becky sat up straight and her eyes shone, although the rest of the class fidgeted and Miss Robertson was still searching for verbs. This wasn't the first time that a horse had come for her, a horse that nobody else could see.

"And what a beauty you are!" she murmured, admiring the chestnut coat that had been brushed and curried until it shone and the long black mane and forelock that curled gracefully over the high forehead. The mare wore a hand-tooled leather saddle and seemed ready for a gallop. Looking directly at Becky, she shook her mane as if to say, "Come on, let's go."

In no time at all she mounted the horse and sat there proud and straight. "Like a princess!" her father had once said about her, and now she felt like a princess, looking down at the room full of squirming classmates. She took the reins, touched her heels to the mare's sides, and made the clicking sound that means "go."

The horse turned gracefully and trotted through the door, down the hall, and out of the school. Picking up speed, she practically flew past the city traffic and in almost no time was galloping through the countryside. Her hoofs sounded pokketa, pokketa, pokketa, like a fast drum tattoo.

The landscape through which the horse galloped resembled the illustrations of storybooks. Wide green hills dotted with daisies and buttercups were clear as watercolors, as were the ferny woods where birds sang in the branches of the trees above and the sun filtered through new green leaves. Now the horse raced across a wide sloping field and slowed down when she came to a blue lake that sparkled under a sky dotted with puffs of cottony clouds. Becky, tall and straight in the saddle, breathed deeply, completely at peace with the world. A reddish path bordered the lake and a gentle pull on the reins sent the mare into an easy canter. Her hoofs sounded a rhythmic clippety-clop, clippety-clop, clippety-clop.

A harsh bell rang, startling as an electric shock. The landscape quivered violently and within a second it vanished, hills, lake, horse, and all. Becky was sitting in the classroom once more.

She straightened her books and stood up. She dreamed of her horse for a minute more, imagining her wandering, stopping to nibble at the tender new grass, and finally, on an impulse, raising her head and galloping over the hills until she was out of sight.

Becky never talked about her horses to anyone. Obviously, adults could not possibly understand and her friends would probably just make fun of her. So if others could not see the horses that came to rescue her from a boring class or an endless session of math, then certainly she would not tell them about the Arabian steeds or the golden palominos.

Yet as Becky walked down the aisle to go to her next class, she felt Miss Robertson looking at her as though she were puzzled.

"Yes, ma'am?" Becky asked politely.

Miss Robertson hesitated, then hedged, asking an ordinary question instead of the one that worried her. "Becky, you do understand all about verbs now, don't you? Grammar is really important, you know."

"Oh yes, Miss Robertson," Becky answered, as though nothing in the world concerned her quite so much as grammar, but there still remained a quizzical look on Miss Robertson's face.

Becky was tempted to reassure her. "Don't worry, Miss Robertson. Everything's all right." But of course she couldn't say that, for then she would have to explain about the chestnut mare and Miss Robertson would never understand. So instead she gave her teacher a warm melting smile. It was the first smile Miss Robertson had received that day and she smiled back gratefully.

Becky's step in the hall was light as she went to the next class. An hour and a half more to go, and then, blessed freedom!

2

Becky Makes a Wish

The last people Becky would have confided in about her afternoon gallop were her two sisters. "Becky's horse" was the family joke, and Mimi and Dori laughed about her passion for horses enough without her urging them for more ridicule.

After school on that mild February day all three girls were jumping rope in front of their house. They had to play in the middle of Hope Street because the sidewalk was covered with trash cans; the garbage collectors hadn't been paid the week before and so they did not come. This had happened before. But Dori said it was better in the street, because there was more space for turning a jump rope even though it meant watching for potholes and scooting out of the way fast when a car came whizzing by.

"My turn, it's my turn!" Mimi yelled, as if she, like Dori, were six years old.

"Oh brother," Becky muttered in disgust. Mimi, almost fourteen, considered herself too dignified to jump rope, and had agreed to do it this time because Dori was so unhappy about her friend's moving away. Yet here she was, more of a baby than Dori, wanting to do all the jumping. Becky stood at one end of the clothesline and Dori at the other, whirling it as fast as they could.

RED HOT PEPPER! One, two, three, four. . . .

"Faster! Faster!" Mimi yelled. Becky put on a last spurt of energy and Mimi missed.

"My turn now!" Dori's voice, usually sweet and high, sounded shrill.

As Mimi and Becky rearranged the ropes so that they could weave the sweeping circles of a double-Dutch jump, which Dori could do forever without missing, Becky noticed that Hope Street seemed more crowded than ever. Everyone seemed to be out catching the last springlike gentleness of the afternoon. It had been a long hard winter during which many people had been unemployed and many families had gone hungry, but the day breathed promise of spring.

"Hello, girls!" It was old Mrs. Horowitz in such a hurry to get home because it was Sabbath that she didn't have time to interrupt their playing to ask how was mother, how was father, and wasn't it a nice day.

Even though it would soon be sundown and the Sabbath would begin, the men walked home from work more slowly than usual, to catch the lingering softness of the late afternoon, and here and there women stopped to chat even though they were in a hurry to get dinner ready. Mothers were calling to their children to come in from the street and get ready for dinner. Becky felt she would like to stay out forever on this lovely day.

A long black car careened down the street, blew its horn impatiently, and then drove on, almost hitting Mimi who had not dashed to the sidewalk quickly enough.

"Phew! That was close!" she said. "But let's not go up yet."

The girls sat on the wooden steps that led up to the porch of the house where they lived. It was a rather ugly three family house. The Goldens lived on the second floor between the Goldsteins on the first and the Kirbys on the

third. Nailed to a post that held up the porch was the sign
that Papa had painted in even gold letters.

RACHEL GOLDEN

DRESSMAKER

Second floor.   Ring bell.

The sign had faded, but it no longer mattered. Everybody
knew Mama. At first only friends in the neighborhood had
come to have their dresses made: Mrs. Rosen, Mrs. Stein,
ancient Mrs. Cohen and her mother who was even more
ancient, Mrs. Spinelli, who lived next door and sang
operatic selections, and her cousin down the street, Mrs.
Nardini. Mama's reputation had spread and now women
came from several blocks away to have their dresses made.

"Hello, girls! It's so nice to see all of you together on this
nice, nice day!" Mrs. Kirby said as she stepped between
Becky and Dori, stopping to pet Dori's head, as she went
upstairs.

Like many people, Mrs. Kirby thought the Golden girls
looked alike. All three were slender with long legs and
vigorous curly black hair which Mrs. Kirby, a hairdresser,
could never stop praising. The girls had a faintly olive cast
to their skin, and therefore it was surprising to find that
their eyes were sometimes blue, sometimes green, but it was
the fringe of black lashes that looked as though charcoal or
mascara had been smeared across their eyelids that gave all
three a certain appearance, known to some as "the Golden
look."

"But we're not alike at all," Mimi had once protested
when she overheard someone discussing them. "Just *look* at
us. We're all different."

As they sat on the stairs that late afternoon, Mimi, with
black hair falling to her waist, might have been an actress

posing for a photograph, sitting with her legs together and her chin held high. Becky could have passed for a boy with the striped baseball cap perched on her crop of short curly hair and the brown corduroy pants a cousin had outgrown and given her. More than once someone had called her "Sonny!" And Dori, though only six, already differed from either of her sisters; a wide-eyed little girl seemingly as fragile as a china doll, she had the strength of fine wire.

Across the street and three houses away, men were loading a moving van. It was only that morning that Margie, Dori's friend, had said a tearful good-by.

"Where did Margie move?" Mimi asked.

"Brookfield, or Brookville. Brook-something."

None of the girls knew where Brook-something was, but each of them imagined it. Becky had never seen much of the country, but she pictured a white house with a herd of horses grazing in the surrounding pastures. Mimi saw a mansion with thick rugs and velvet drapes and a grand piano, while Dori dreamed of a sweet little cottage with ruffly curtains and downy little ducks and geese swimming on a pond nearby.

The front window on the second floor opened with a squeak and the rich low voice of Mrs. Golden interrupted her daughters' reveries. She spoke with an accent that might have been Russian or Jewish.

"Time to come up, Mimi. You too, Becky and Dori."

"Aw, Mama, not yet! It's nice out."

"Ten minutes more, Mom. Just ten minutes?" Dori begged.

"Well," Mrs. Golden seemed to think it over, "all right, ten minutes but no more. It's Sabbath. Your father will be home soon and we're having company."

The window shut and the girls watched the moving men carry out a table.

"I wish I were moving," Mimi said, dreaming.

"Not me," Dori said. "I wouldn't want to move at all, not even to be with Margie. Papa said we belong on Hope Street. We've always been here."

"And we always will," Mimi said, "as long as he keeps getting laid off."

"But he's got a job," Becky said, defending her father. "He's been working for a week now."

"Look at that sign. That's the truth of it," Mimi said.

Someone had written in letters on the street sign so that it now read "Hopeless Street."

"Anyway, it's where I live," Dori said righteously, defending it.

The sounds of Bobby Goldstein's piano practice drifted through the twilight, and that too was part of Hope Street. Bobby was playing "Welcome Sweet Springtime," and although he sometimes forgot to include the sharps or the flats, the song was familiar, as familiar as the street and the houses they had always known.

Hope Street had never been one of those dignified streets that had later become run down. It had always been ugly, even when new, a short street lined with bulky three-story houses of wood, brick, or stucco. Every year these houses grew even less appealing as the paint peeled off, bricks became mysteriously chipped or broken, and windows were sometimes covered with boards because it was too expensive to replace the broken glass. Mama had tried to grow roses in the tiny yard below, but they always weakened, turned yellow, and died. Daisies and sunflowers, which had the reputation of being able to grow anywhere, took the place of the roses. But children playing stamped over the new green shoots of the sunflowers, and they died too.

Still, it was home.

The window upstairs opened again and this time Mama had to say only one word. "Girls!"

"We're coming," Mimi called back.

They stood up reluctantly and it was then that Becky noticed the first star as it glowed in the sky. It had appeared unnoticed while they talked.

"Look," Becky cried, "the first star!"

And without waiting, she closed her eyes and recited the magic verse.

> Star light, star bright,
> First star I see tonight.
> Wish I may, wish I might
> Have the wish I wish tonight.

She closed her eyes to make a wish and instantly saw herself trotting along the beach on a golden horse. Her sisters took a little longer.

"What'd you wish for?" Dori asked.

"Can't tell. It won't come true."

"But I *know* what you wished for, and Mimi too," Dori said smugly with that maddening exactness that Becky couldn't stand. But before she could put her hand over Dori's mouth, Dori cried, "Becky wants a horse and Mimi wants to be a blonde!"

"Brat!" Mimi cried, for of course Dori had been right. "And I know about you too. You want Margie back."

"Maybe yes, maybe no," Dori admitted, "but what I really wish is that we'd all have dinner soon because I'm starving. Last one up is a rotten egg!" she cried as she started up the stairs. Mimi followed but Becky lingered.

Wishes were strange, she thought. They had to be chosen carefully. It would be silly to wish for dinner if you were getting it anyway, or to wish for blonde hair when you were born with pitch black locks; but then, wasn't it silly to wish for a *dream* horse, when you could dream about horses any time. Now then, what if she were to wish for a real horse?

A *real horse?* But that was ridiculous, absurd, utterly impossible. A live horse on Hope Street? And yet. . . .

Impulsively she turned to the evening star once more, closed her eyes, said the verse quickly, and this time she wished for a real horse.

Then drawing in her breath sharply, she turned and ran up the stairs into the house.

3

Uncle Jonas Visits

The minute Becky bounced into the kitchen, she was aware of the special Sabbath feeling that came to the Golden household every Friday evening. It wasn't only the fragrance that came from the stove or the scrubbed polished look of the kitchen, but a very particular feeling that suggested something else which could not be seen or defined but which made this night more sacred than other nights.

Becky pulled out a wooden kitchen chair and sat backward on it, her long legs stretching out on either side and her chin resting on the back of the chair where she folded her arms. From that position she watched Mama hurrying around the kitchen, seeming to do a hundred last-minute things at once. Her face was flushed with the heat of the oven and the excitement of company coming. At the last moment she was mending a tiny hole she had just noticed in one of the worn damask napkins, hurrying in the last light of day because she wasn't supposed to sew on the Sabbath.

"Mimi, would you please get out the brass polish and go over the candlesticks?" she asked, although the ancient brass candlesticks that had come with her from Russia were already gleaming.

Becky shook her head. Everything had to be perfect where Mama was concerned. On Fridays she put away her sewing machine, no matter how much she preferred sewing to cleaning, and she spent the entire day scrubbing, cleaning, polishing the house, and cooking. Somehow she managed to transform the old familiar rooms into something that Becky always saw as shining and golden.

The color gold was everywhere, in the brass candlesticks that held the two white candles, in the shiny copper teapot, and in the roast chicken Mama had just taken from the oven so she could sprinkle red paprika over its shining surface. Its odor drifted across the room to Becky.

"I'm starving," she said. "I won't last till dinner."

"And I won't either," Dori said, laying a finger on the *challeh,* the braided bread Mama made each Friday for the Sabbath. The shiny golden crust was covered with tiny black poppy seeds and its fragrance was more than Becky or Dori could stand. Mama read their minds.

She shook her head gently. "No, darling, I know you're hungry and you too, Becky. No wonder, you're both growing up so fast! But it would not be very nice for Papa to bless bread with two slices missing, would it?"

The girls understood and Mama changed the subject.

"Dori, I ironed your new blue dress. Would you like to wear it tonight? And Becky, it wouldn't hurt you to put on a dress too, all right? On Sabbath, you should wear a dress."

Dori ran off, a glutton for new clothes. But Becky did not move.

"It's hypocritical," she said.

"It's hypocritical to wear a dress?" Mama asked. "What is that supposed to mean?" She spoke absently, as she was tasting the soup to see if it needed more salt.

"Mama, every day when I get home from school I put on pants. Why? Because it seems right. If I put on a dress, it's pretending I'm someone else."

Mama sighed. How could Becky bring up arguments

when she was so busy, and such silly arguments as they were. "It would hurt you to be 'hypocritical' when you look so nice in a dress? That red dress is made just for you, nobody else. Besides there's company tonight."

"Who?"

"Aunt Clara, Joey, and Sylvia—Uncle Charlie's away this weekend. And old Aunt Martha is coming and Cousin Berenice."

"Cousin Berenice? Oh no!" Becky cried, and jumping off the chair began to imitate Cousin Berenice, her father's charmless cousin, a schoolteacher with an overdeveloped sense of what was right and what was wrong. "Oh, and this is little Becky? I thought it might be some young boy with that short hair and those pants, but now I do see, it really is little Becky!" Becky imitated Cousin Berenice perfectly, even remembering to sniff and finish her sentence with a nod as though to emphasize that she had indeed spoken. Mimi laughed with appreciation, and although Mama cried, "Oh Becky, you shouldn't make fun of that poor lady. She means well!" Mama had a hard time hiding a smile.

"Becky, please, will you see if I put enough napkins on the table? I don't remember." It was Mama's way of changing a subject when she did not really want to scold Becky.

Becky, alone in the dining room, counted the napkins and that done, she hesitated. The evening promised little. Mimi and Sylvia would whisper secrets and not let her join them. Joey would pester her with riddles but would play with Dori. And so she would be alone.

Alone, yet everyone would be there. The Sabbath table wore the familiar Sabbath look. The linen tablecloth, mended over and over again, had taken on a silvery sheen with its many washings. The decanter of wine that stood near Papa's place glowed as though it were lit from within.

The Sabbath candles waited serenely and the braided loaf of bread rested under its special embroidered cloth.

She felt a sudden chill on her back and turning around she could see that a hostile wind had arisen. Outside the dark had come swiftly and without knowing why, she shivered. Then she drew the curtains together and pulled down the shades. There, that was better. The waiting dining room was quietly lit, like a scene in a play.

The telephone rang. She heard Mama answering it in the kitchen and in the next moment heard her mother say, "Jonas, you're in town? What a nice surprise! You'll have to come over for dinner!"

Pause.

"Of course it's not too much trouble. I'll put another cup of water in the soup! Come right over."

Uncle Jonas was in town! Becky's eyes lit up. Of course that part about Mama's putting an extra cup of water in the soup was a family joke. Mama could never turn down anyone who might be hungry or lonely. She had a knack for stretching a dinner for four until it could serve twelve.

"Is he really coming?" Becky cried.

"Yes, darling. So now, would you like to put on a dress?"

Without a word, Becky rushed to the bedroom to pull off her shirt and pants; in honor of Uncle Jonas, Becky scrubbed her face until it turned pink. She put on the red dress with its embroidered bodice because she knew Uncle Jonas liked it, and she begged Mimi to lend her an outgrown pair of black patent leather shoes. She hadn't quite finished brushing her hair when she heard the doorbell ring.

Uncle Jonas was not really an uncle, but a mysteriously related person on her mother's side, a man who stood on the outer fringes of a large family. Dori had once heard Aunt

Clara say that he was a black sheep. Although Mama later
had insisted that of course he wasn't a black sheep, Becky
still felt that he was a little different from the rest of the
family and she felt sometimes that she too was apart in some
ways. But the real bond between them, other than that
mysterious liking that happens between people, was that
Uncle Jonas liked horses.

Becky liked his mysteriousness. Nobody knew where he
lived, although Mama thought it was in Boston and Aunt
Clara suspected it was Providence, not far from the race
track. Nobody knew what his business was nor if he had a
wife or any personal family. He simply showed up now and
then, a tiny man with a worn briefcase under his arm and
always an unexpected hat. One time it might be a Sherlock
Holmes cap and the next a furry beaver, or a dashing
borsalino, like the hats worn in gangster films.

His very presence upset grownups, particularly Cousin
Berenice who found him improper in every way, but as he
himself said, dogs and children loved him enough to make
up for all the adults who didn't.

When Becky heard the doorbell ring, she ran to open it
and there he was, tiny Uncle Jonas, wearing a French beret
and carrying a single rose for Mrs. Golden, as was his
custom. Becky could not tell if his small blue eyes overlaid
with wrinkles were twinkling with amusement or if they
were uncommonly sad, or perhaps both.

"You're just the same!" Becky cried, "only a little
smaller."

"No, Becky, it's you that's taller!" he answered. Then
they embraced and in the next minute everyone seemed to
have arrived. Cousin Berenice could not stop remarking
about Becky's being in a dress, and Becky tried not to laugh
when Mimi winked.

Suddenly Becky felt happy to have a houseful of loving people. She even felt grateful for Cousin Berenice. But it was Uncle Jonas she sat beside at dinner.

The evening passed as quickly as a dream and in its quiet way it had the feeling of something not quite real. The mildness of the day had changed to a night of savage wind, as though bad spirits were menacing outside the windows.

Soon after everyone arrived they sat at the table and repeated the same solemn beautiful Sabbath ceremony that Becky had heard since she was a baby. Mama put a soft kerchief on her head as she said the brief Hebrew prayer and lit the Sabbath candles. Then Papa stood up with the silver blessing cup in his hand and he drank the wine after repeating the blessings. The fragrant bread was sliced, and then Becky and Mimi brought in the steaming bowls of chicken soup.

"I hear that you are working again," Aunt Clara said. Papa nodded.

"Yes, thank God. I was lucky to find something again. Watchmakers are a funny breed. They aren't needed very much, but you can't live without them either. So I hope my luck holds. It's good to be working again."

"You're lucky," Aunt Clara said. "Here it is 1938 already and you still see grown men, who should be working, selling apples for a nickel, or pencils."

"Or poor ragged souls who come to your door and ask if they can't work for you in exchange for a meal," Berenice said.

"Well, bad as it is here, it's worse in Europe."

"Europe? Don't mention it. It's too awful. Anyway, we don't know."

The conversation had become heavy, and Becky knew

that it distressed Mama. It was all right for Mama to have a
rule in her own family that unhappy matters must wait until
after dinner, but she could not tell that to her guests.
Instead she changed the subject.

"Aunt Martha, do you know what? I have made *kasha* for
you, because I know you love it."

"Thank you, Rachel. I do. Since I was a child in Russia, I
have liked it, and the way you make it is like my mother
used to make it."

Kasha was made of buckwheat groats, and it was
something like rice or barley. Becky wasn't very fond of it,
but at least it changed the conversation. Now the talk
turned to the old tales of their childhood in Russia. Clearing
away the soup plates and bringing on the rest of the dinner,
Becky wondered why they repeated the same stories again
and again.

"Remember the time we went on a sleigh ride?" Aunt
Clara asked Becky's father. "How old Reuben borrowed the
sleigh, I don't know, but it was so cold that night, with the
stars twinkling. And I was so afraid of the wolves!"

"In Russia it wasn't the wolves one had to be afraid of. It
was the pogroms," Aunt Martha said in her slow ancient
voice. She did not speak often, but when she did, everyone
listened.

"What's a pogrom?" Dori asked in her sweet high voice.
Mama looked pained. How could one talk of such things
and enjoy a meal? Yet she said nothing and Aunt Martha
explained.

"A pogrom was when the Russians or Tartars would raid
a Jewish village or a ghetto. They did such terrible things,
Dori, I can hardly bear to tell you. They would steal, and
kill people, and trample them down under their horses, set
the houses on fire—awful, awful things."

"But why did they want to do that?" Dori asked. Becky felt as if somehow she had always known without having to ask.

"For many reasons," Uncle Jonas said, "but mostly, little Dori, because the peasants were sometimes so miserable that it made them feel better to kick someone else who couldn't fight back, like the Jews. Maybe some of them were bored and it amused them to raid a village."

"But that's awful!" Dori said. "Did they kill .children too?"

"Sometimes they tried. But more than once we got away," Papa said, trying to get away now from the dismal memories. "But when things went well—that is to say, when we were not starving or being murdered—then sometimes I had fun, mostly with Bernard, when we were boys together."

Mimi winked at Becky for they knew the old story that Papa had told countless times. Once Mimi had repeated it with him, word for word. But this time she waited politely as her father spoke.

"We used to live near the river, and what a river it was, as clean and swift and cold as you'd ever want to see. The fish in that river were like this."

He held up his hands to show how big they were. Each time he told the story the fish became larger by at least an inch.

"And my cousin Bernard—what friends we were—we used to go fishing when we could and every day we would swim, even when we didn't feel like it. One day the snow was blowing and it was freezing, but we were stubborn and Bernard dared me to go swimming. You know how foolish boys are. So I went in, and the water was so cold I began to freeze; I couldn't breathe and I was getting a cramp from the extreme cold. So Bernard jumped in, from the bridge, mind you, and he managed to save me. He risked his own life, of course. The crazy things kids do." He smiled as he finished, but the smile was half sad.

"Speaking of Bernard," Aunt Clara said, "have you heard from him?"

Papa became solemn. "Yes." He did not want to talk about it but Aunt Clara went on.

"What does he say?"

"What can he say?" Papa thundered, almost as if he were angry. "Hitler gave an ultimatum in January to Austria; Austria is full of Nazis, enough to make a difference. And Hitler may take over any time. Then it will be like it is in Germany. Right now, Bernard still has an important job in the symphony. He is their best violinist. And his wife, Anna, is a lovely person; this I know. And they are very proud of their little boy, David. But there's fear in that letter. And to tell you the truth, I'm afraid, too, of that madman, Hitler, and what he can do."

"There's never an end to it," Aunt Clara whispered, hoping the children wouldn't hear, "and the unspeakable things they are doing to the Jews in Germany. Unspeakable."

Everyone had stopped eating. Even Joey and Dori who had been giggling over some secret joke became quiet. Becky wanted to shut out all the talk. She knew what was happening. She knew that Hitler wanted to kill them all. His shrieking hysterical voice on the radio had filled her with terror even though she did not understand a word of German. When he spoke she fled from the house, not wanting to listen or to think about him.

Becky's mother looked around the table and Becky knew she was not at all happy with the conversation.

"Come," she said, "it's Sabbath and we must give thanks because we are all together and we must pray for those poor souls who are suffering. But Joey, I haven't heard a word out of you? How are the clarinet lessons, h'm? And how about another piece of chicken for you. Berenice, more carrot pudding? And Jonas, I know how you love noodles. Come, help yourself. Please. Martha, I meant to tell you, that dress is so becoming."

Mama was awkward, Becky thought, but everyone understood. Then Uncle Jonas tried to cheer everyone up with a little anecdote about Mama's cooking when she was a young bride. The conversation was awkward, but it was better than getting morbid over Europe. Becky was glad that Europe and Germany and Austria were three thousand miles away.

Looking into the flames of the candles, she saw a tiny horse in each. On one horse she placed an imaginary Cousin Bernard with Anna and David and set them galloping out of sight. And on the other horse, she saw a miniature Becky on a miniature circus horse and they rode proudly around and around until it was time to help Mama clear the dinner dishes and bring on the chocolate cake Aunt Clara had brought for dessert.

After dinner the company moved to the tiny living room and Becky sat on the edge of the overstuffed chair where Uncle Jonas sat.

"Hello, Becky. Now we can talk a little. I think there's something on your mind?" Becky was almost tempted to tell him about her wish for the horse. Certainly he was the only person who would not make fun of her for liking horses or would not tell her to be more sensible. Still, if she talked about her wish, it wouldn't come true. But she could ask questions.

"Well, I'd like to know how much horses cost."

She was relieved when he did not laugh at her but answered seriously.

"It depends on what kind of horse you want. An old wornout plug might go for fifteen or twenty dollars if the dogfood companies don't get there first. And race horses sell anywhere in the thousands. There are different kinds of horses at different prices. Why, are you going to buy a horse, Becky?"

"Of course not. I was only curious."

"A good riding horse might be found for one or two hundred dollars. But that's only the beginning. You have to keep him somewhere. You have to feed him. You need a stable, straw, horse shoes, and now and then a veterinarian. You still like horses, eh, Becky?"

His eyes, although sympathetic, suggested the tiniest hint of amusement. So Becky took a lesson from her mother and changed the subject.

"Did you ever know Cousin Bernard?" she whispered.

He nodded gravely. Even though Uncle Jonas was from Mama's side of the family, Becky had the feeling that he knew everyone and had been everywhere. His voice became serious and wistful as he answered her.

"I didn't know Bernard personally, but I was in Vienna some time ago and I heard him play his violin. What a genius he is! He plays like an angel. And I had the idea he might be one too, or at least a very fine man. He is someone you could never forget. There's an expression 'kissed by the angels' and maybe he was.

"And Vienna itself," Uncle Jonas leaned back and with his eyes half closed began to speak about the city he had once loved.

"I wish you could have seen it then, when I was there. A city of music with opera and theater and concerts all the time, and fine palaces, beautiful women, as I recall; at least some of them were very beautiful. They had style. And there were coffee houses where you could sit for hours and drink *kaffe it schlag*—that's whipped cream—and then the pastry shops. Oh Becky!" he patted his flat stomach as though he had a paunch. "And the people I knew there. The conversations were so good; you could talk for hours about everything. And the music, the Mozart and the Beethoven and the Strauss waltzes."

He sighed heavily and Becky could see that Uncle Jonas, who was always smiling, was not smiling now. "It's all gone, Becky, all gone for us. And for others too. These are fearful times we live in, my dear."

But the worry on Becky's face upset him. There will be enough time to worry, Uncle Jonas thought to himself, and changed the subject. "Let me tell you about the famous white stallions, the Lippizaner horses. Have you heard of them?"

And so the evening flew. The company left all at once and Becky, exhausted, fell asleep, dreaming of the proud Lippizaner horses that Uncle Jonas had seen so long ago.

4

A Troublesome Wish

By Saturday the weather was normal once more, which meant that February returned to its gray bleakness without even the grace of soft falling snow. A freezing dismal February weekend.

From time to time, every now and then, Becky remembered the wish she had made. "It really wasn't very bright," she chided herself. How could she keep a horse? Where? Never was there a more impossible desire. Yet the wish stayed with her stubbornly. It was there, like a fact, and it did little good to be sensible and try to forget it.

On Monday morning she was still thinking about it.

"Becky, you're dawdling. Hurry with your breakfast. School!" her mother said.

She took a spoonful of hot cereal to pacify her mother. But while her parents chattered, Mimi was finishing homework, and Dori was reading the cereal box, Becky continued the dialog with herself. How to get a horse.

One thing was certain. One did not ask one's parents, not if one was in the Golden family. Not only did Papa find it difficult to pay the rent and grocery bills, but even if he had money, he wouldn't understand about Becky's horse. She could see him blink his eyes as though astounded.

"A horse, Becky, a HORSE? Did I hear right? You said

you wanted me to buy you a horse. That's just what I've
been waiting to hear. It's so easy to find shoes for five pair of
feet that I can't wait to get a horse who'll need two pair of
shoes. To say nothing of oats and a stable. So you can ride
your horse to school. Ah Becky, you've got a sense of
humor!"

He would laugh and chuck her under the chin, because of
course he would take it as a joke. If he thought for one
moment that she was serious, he would take her to a doctor.
"There's something wrong with her head," he would say.

"All right, so we don't ask Papa. We don't go out and buy
a horse."

An ordinary wish would be granted in just such an
ordinary way, but this wish was very special.

"Becky, you'll never get through school if you don't eat
your breakfast. Your cocoa's getting cold. Are you sure
you're all right, darling?"

As Becky hastened to drink her chocolate, she thought of
Uncle Alexander, the rich uncle. He was so rich he couldn't
begin to count all his money and he loved his three nieces.
There was nothing he would not give them. More than once
Becky, Mimi, and Dori had lain in their beds and dreamed
of the cars, dresses, and jewelry that Uncle Alexander was
going to give them. He would be more than happy to give
Becky a palomino for her birthday.

If only Uncle Alexander were real! Unfortunately he
came from the imaginations of Becky and Mimi, and the
horse he would so gladly give Becky would be as lovely but
unreal as the horses she already owned.

Well then, perhaps she would save a child from a burning
building, or snatch a toddler from the wheels of an
onrushing car, or jump in a river to rescue a drowning little
boy, and the grateful parents would give her whatever she
wanted. It was all chancey, but not impossible.

"Becky, I don't know what's got into you. You'll be late for school. And you forget to give me your gloves. I want to mend that little hole in your finger. Here, darling, I can do it for you now. It will only be a second."

The drowning child, the grateful parents, the medal of honor she would receive from the mayor, and the horse that would come to her as a gift vanished, and the world rushed in. She had to finish breakfast, find the gloves so Mama could mend them, finish her arithmetic homework, and remember to pick up her friend, Lisa Kline, on the way to school.

She sighed. Her horse was still a dream.

5

A Letter Comes from Vienna

The wind had been so biting and sharp that Becky and Lisa had raced all the way home from school. In spite of the wind they would have stood on the corner chatting for half an hour, as they did every other day, but Lisa had to go to ballet classes. "Or else I'll lose my scholarship!" she said.

"Hoity-toit, so I'll lose my scholarship!" Becky imitated her as she ran home the rest of the way. Lisa could put on airs when she chose, but even so, she was a good friend. Becky forgave her.

"Hey Mother, I'm home!" Becky called from the kitchen.

It took only a second for Mrs. Golden to remove the pins from her mouth and call back to her daughter.

"Hello, darling. I'm in the bedroom, Becky, fitting Mrs. Gorski to her lovely blue woolen dress!"

This seemingly innocent statement was a disguise message for the girls to stay out of the bedroom for the moment. Customers did not appreciate Mama's slim daughters coming in as they stood in corsets and slips while Mama tacked sleeves and bodices together on them.

Becky would have liked to change from her school dress to pants and a sweater, but that could wait. She poured a glass of milk for herself and reached in the cookie jar for three of Mama's raisin cookies. How good they were, she thought. When Papa worked, Mama made such good things to eat, and when Papa was out of work—but she didn't want to think about it.

She sat at the kitchen table, leafed idly through a magazine, and then her spirits fell as she noticed the letter propped up against the sugar bowl. The thin writing paper, the delicate foreign script, and the stamps with the menacing black bird and the word Osterreich, which was German for Austria, meant that the letter addressed to Papa was from Cousin Bernard.

She knew exactly what would happen. Her father would come home from work, as usual, and he would be in good spirits, joking with Mimi, tousling Becky's short black curly hair, and lifting Dori high in the air. Then he would see the letter, would fold it and put it in his pocket, and become silent and withdrawn that night and for the next few days.

"Sometimes I wish I never had a Cousin Bernard," she said to herself.

"Then where would you be, because it was Bernard who rescued your father from drowning?"

"Then I'd be someone else," she answered. And what a strange idea that was! Anyway, she couldn't imagine anyone else but Papa as her father. And she didn't really mind Cousin Bernard; for heaven's sake she didn't even *know* him. It was just that his letters made her father so worried and withdrawn that he didn't even notice his daughters for several days.

Suddenly Becky wanted to get away from that letter. She put on her jacket, called to her mother, "I'm going to the library, Mom!" and ran down the stairs. Perhaps there'd be a new horse book and she wouldn't have to think about the letter.

It happened exactly as Becky predicted. Papa came home joking and telling some stories he had heard at work, and then Mama gave him the letter. Everything changed. The family ate their borscht silently as they sat around the kitchen table for dinner. Even Dori's bright chatter seemed to fade away.

When the dishes were done and the kitchen table scrubbed, Papa said he had work to do. Becky, sitting across the table from him, watched him lay down the sheet of ground glass on which he worked and then place his tools along the edge of the glass in orderly progression: the tiny screwdrivers, the small files, the tweezers, and the small metal boxes in which the tiny parts of the watch were kept. Papa was a logical man. Becky loved watching him work. His hands seemed large and powerful, yet they handled the delicate springs and wheels of the tiny gold watch with skill. Although Becky could have touched him, he seemed to be many miles away. At last she spoke. "Papa."

He looked up at her. The jeweler's magnifying glass he wore over one eye made it seem large.

"Papa, what was in that letter from Bernard?"

"Here, read it yourself," he said, taking it from his pocket.

"In Russian, Papa? Or Yiddish? You know I don't understand."

"I forgot. Well, I'll tell you, Becky, he doesn't say much. It's what he doesn't say that bothers me. On the surface, everything is all right. He still plays in the Symphony Orchestra, but he has noticed they don't play the work of Jewish composers any more. What kind of nonsense is that? He says that his wife, Anna, and David are studying music together and David seems talented; that part is all right. But he mentions that a string quartet he played in doesn't seem to meet any more. Why, Becky, when they were doing very well? Many of his friends, he writes, have gone away. And he wishes with all his heart he could see all of us."

"That's not so very bad, is it, Papa?"

"Not yet. I keep saying those words, 'not yet,' but I'm afraid things will get worse. What about his friends who 'go away' so mysteriously, or does he mean they were forced to leave? Well, it's hard to know. Even the refugees from Germany I have met cannot tell us everything that is going on."

"What exactly do we know?"

"Some things we do know. Hitler means to conquer the world; he's written it, he shouts it all the time. And he means to get rid of the Jews. Even when he was beginning, his brown-shirt gangsters used to beat up Jews, destroy Jewish businesses, and destroy the synagogues. Then there was a boycott against Jewish stores. Jews had to register all their property. They had to give up the right of citizenship. Heaven alone knows what else went on, or still goes on for that matter. Some escape and others stay on, thinking it can't get worse."

"Can it get worse?"

Papa's face was full of sorrow as he looked at Becky. "Yes, it can get worse. We know that from history. I have heard that sometimes there is a knock on the door in the middle of the night and there are the secret police; they make the victims dress, they take them away, and nobody ever hears from them again. It's an age of terror."

"But why, Papa? Why do they pick on the Jews?"

Papa put down his jeweler's eyepiece and rubbed his forehead. Becky had never seen him look so troubled. "Maybe it's our fate. They say we're the chosen ones; maybe this is what we're chosen for. Maybe it makes our tormentors feel better about their own lives if they can persecute and kill us, destroy us."

"But we've survived, Papa. We're still here. And I just can't think of us not surviving."

Papa nodded. "That I believe too. We shall survive even this. But with such pain, such sorrow, such needless torture."

"If only there were something we could do about it."

"We could have a country of our own. Zion. It's the dream of our people."

"Do you think it will ever happen, Papa? It's such a big thing to wish."

"Sure, Becky, I do believe it. How or when it will happen, I don't know. And it won't be easy, that I do know. But when so many people want a home and need a home, then sooner or later, the dream will come true. I hope I live to see it."

"And now, before we settle all the problems of the world in one night, will you let me get to work on this watch? It's a special order and must be finished by tomorrow morning. Come to think of it, don't you ever have any homework?"

Becky nodded, slipped off her chair, and put her arms around her father as she kissed him goodnight. And as she did her homework, sitting on her bed, she looked up from her book with a new thought, "If father can wish for a whole country, and my father's a reasonable man, then perhaps it's all right for me to wish for a horse. Well, isn't it?"

6

Hair

On a Sunday night while Becky sat on her narrow bed and drew horses in a blue-lined composition book, Mimi was at her dressing table, frowning at the image in the small oval mirror that hung over it. She was wearing the flowered robe which Mama had made for her. The "dressing table" flaunted a gauzy skirt drawn up at regular intervals with dainty velvet bows. Mama had cleverly made the table from two orange crates with boards nailed across the top, and with a pair of patched curtains, made the misty skirt around it, using the new velvet ribbon bows to hold the ragged parts together. The dainty mirror above the dressing table had once been a chipped castoff in a junk shop.

Becky, looking up from her drawing, watched Mimi brushing her hair and realized almost with surprise that her sister was becoming very pretty. Had she never noticed it before, or was this some new mysterious blooming? Mimi's olive skin seemed to have taken on a pink glow that wasn't there before and the black hair that fell down her back seemed richer and blacker than ever.

"Your hair sure is long. Like a horse's tail," Becky said.

Mimi was insulted. She fumed. "At least it's not a mop like yours."

"I was complimenting you, dummy," Becky explained. "I mean your hair looks gorgeous, like the tail of a five thousand dollar show horse. Well, maybe only a four thousand dollar horse."

Mimi's frown disappeared. Frowning was bad for the forehead, she reminded herself. "Thanks," she said to Becky uncertainly. Mama had always said that if you didn't know whether a remark was a compliment or an insult, it's best to consider it a compliment.

Becky returned to her drawing, muttering about the difficulties of making a horse's legs bend the right way. When she looked up at Mimi again, Mimi was involved in a ritual that consisted of pushing up the tip of her nose one hundred times each night in the belief that if she did this often enough, her nose would take the hint and become shorter.

"Your nose isn't all that bad," Becky said. "I don't know why you worry about it. What's wrong with a long nose? Mine's only a little shorter than yours, but I don't worry."

"You just don't understand anything about noses," Mimi said. "If only you could see Barbara Bentley's nose. It's the most adorable little nose. It turns up in the air, just so!"

"I've seen it and I don't think it's so adorable," Becky answered. "Looks to me like she's smelling something bad."

Becky had seen Barbara only once and had detested her, yet it was not so much Barbara herself as her effect on Mimi that bothered her. Mimi, usually sensible, adored Barbara and followed her around like a little sheep. Barbara had moved from Boston three months ago and had the added glamor of being new. Becky wished she had stayed in Boston. It was "Barbara this" and "Barbara that" from Mimi until Becky wanted to scream.

"I could forget about my nose, if it weren't for my hair," Mimi said, talking more to herself than to her sister. "Everyone's got black hair and I'm sick of it. If only I were blonde like Barbara, I'd live and die happy. I'd never ask for another thing in my life."

"Oh yes you would. Anyway, you can't change things like the color of your hair. If you're born with black hair and a long nose, then that's it."

"Changing the color of your hair isn't as crazy as wanting a horse," Mimi shot back. "Who do you think you are, Mrs. Vanderbilt or someone?"

Becky withdrew in silence. If secret wishes remained secret, there'd be fewer arguments. But when you shared a room with a sister, there weren't any secrets.

"Have you ever really looked at Barbara's hair?" The dreamy tone came back into Mimi's voice. "It's pale gold with just a little curl at the ends, and it's long, down past her waist. Like mine. Only she has about three hundred ribbons and scarves to dress it up. And lights all around the mirror of her dressing table, like a theater dressing room."

"I hate Barbara Bentley," Becky mumbled in a low voice, but Mimi went on, like an actress with the spotlight on her.

"She has a canary in a little gold cage and her own little radio in her room. Her bedroom is all in pink, everything pink, even the sheets on her bed. And a little white fur rug that's so soft. And in the living room, there's a tremendous radio that lights up in colors when it's on."

"How come you always go to her house and she never comes here? You ashamed of us?" Becky asked as she filled in the outlines of her drawing, the horse's legs at last having bent correctly. She did not see the quick look that Mimi darted at her, indicating that Becky had come closer to the truth than she had realized.

"Of course I'm not ashamed, silly. But you know, Mama's always got customers coming in for fittings and she doesn't want us in the way," she ended self-righteously.

But the truth was, she would not have dared invite Barbara home. To bring the elegant Barbara to dismal Hope Street and up the stairs to their house which was clean but somehow so worn and plain, and the sounds of Bobby

Goldstein's awful piano, and the neighbors fighting which
could be heard so easily when the wind was right—all that
was unthinkable. But the real reason she never invited
Barbara home was Mama. Mama spoke with an accent,
although it wasn't until she met Barbara that Mimi realized
it. Barbara thought all accents were dreadful excepting a
Boston or a British accent, which was, of course, superior.
Mama's accent was hardly British; whether it was Russian
or Yiddish, Mimi wasn't sure, but Mama's voice was so low
and calm that Papa once described it as being as rich as fruit
cake soaked in honey.

Once when Mimi and Barbara were walking to the
library, they met Mrs. Wilensky, one of Mama's friends. She
greeted Mimi with a cordial hello and asked how Mama was
in a marked accent. They had hardly said good-by when
Barbara made a face and burst out laughing. "You do know
some odd characters, don't you?" she had asked Mimi.

For an insane moment, Mimi had wanted to slap
Barbara's face and walk away. Insulting Mrs. Wilensky for
her accent was like insulting Mama. But Mimi hesitated,
and with the hesitation came the excuses. Barbara had
never met Mama and if she had, she wouldn't laugh at her;
Mimi was being oversensitive and decided to let it pass this
time.

While she was thinking about this, Mama called from the
kitchen. "Girls, darlings, it's time to go to sleep now. You
have school tomorrow."

"There," Mimi thought, "she really does have an accent."
The *s* of girls should have sounded like a *z* and not an *s;*
sleeping sounded like *slipping;* and *darlings* sounded like
darlinks. Although Mimi was justified in noticing the accent,
she also realized she was somewhat embarrassed by it.

Half an hour later, although the lights had long since been
turned out and goodnights said, each girl lay in her bed
wide awake.

"Mimi, are you sleeping?"

"No. Are you?"

"Not really. Listen, Mimi, don't do it."

"Don't do what?" Mimi asked although she knew.

"Your hair. Leave it alone. Okay?"

"Barbara wants to dye it for me. There's lots of peroxide in their house because her mother is always bleaching her hair, and well, I'd like to try it."

"Papa would kill you. He really would. He loves your hair just the way it is and anyway, he hates bleached blondes."

"It's my hair, not Papa's."

"That's not the point."

"Yes, it is."

"No, it isn't. It's awfully clear, Mimi. You don't want to look Jewish. You want to be a Barbara Bentley, and you can't, because you're not."

It was a touchy moment. "Barbara looks elegant. She doesn't live in a slum like Hope Street. And she doesn't have to worry about relatives in Europe. Or her father being out of a job. Everyone I know worries about relatives in Germany and Austria. It's such a drag."

No sooner had she said this, then she was ashamed, but she had started and could not stop. Becky answered in a voice so calm and soft, it was almost like Mama's.

"You are what you are, Mimi. It's there. It will always be there. You can't hide it or cover it up or become a Barbara Bentley. Anyway, you're really handsome and she's just a little nothing."

Mimi could not handle her conflicting loyalties and her temper flared up.

"Barbara is not a 'nothing' and if I want to dye my hair, then I will."

"I'll bet you wouldn't dare."

"I'll bet I would."

Becky could have bitten her lip. She knew she had said

the one thing that would drive Mimi to bleaching her hair.
Mimi took bets seriously and had only contempt for anyone
who didn't.

"What will you bet, Becky? You started it. You can't back
out."

"My gold locket, I guess," Becky said, swallowing hard.
She was taking a chance. This gold locket, the sole heirloom
of her mother's mother who had been killed in a pogrom in
Russia was her dearest treasure. Mimi would not really want
to take it. She recognized Becky's strategy.

"You shouldn't bet on something like that," she scolded
Becky. "You wouldn't want to give that up." And then,
unable somehow to back down, she made a proposal almost
as disastrous.

"I'll bet my new angora sweater."

The situation seemed hopeless. Mimi had saved her
allowance for months, had gone without lunches at school
and had taken on any baby-sitting jobs she could find in
order to buy her precious angora sweater. Becky would no
more think of taking her sweater than Mimi would take the
locket.

On the other hand, a bet was a kind of promise. If only
I'd kept quiet, Becky thought.

It was then that the door opened and Mr. Golden peered
into the dark room. "And when you ladies have finished
your conversation, do you suppose you could take a little
sleep?" Becky felt the love in his voice coming through the
half-joking reprimand. When he was safely out of earshot,
she whispered:

"Mimi, let's call off the bet. I will if you will. Don't touch
your hair. Leave it the way it is, OK?"

Mimi bit her lip. "It's bad luck to unmake a bet. But we
can put a two week limit on it."

Becky had never heard about its being bad luck to call off

a bet and she suspected Mimi had made up this superstition. Yet going through the arguments again would only make Mimi all the more stubborn.

Deeply troubled, both girls finally fell asleep.

7

The Bet

As the first tense week passed, both Becky and Mimi carefully avoided the word "hair." Neither girl had forgotten the bet, but they did not dare to mention it. Becky knew that a word from her would send Mimi flying to Barbara's to get the deed done. So she kept quiet and hoped the whole matter would pass forgotten.

As the first days of the second week passed and Mimi still appeared with her hair as black and luxuriant as ever, Becky breathed more easily and almost stopped worrying. Besides, the gym teacher had asked her to help arrange a track meet and that kept her busy enough that she had little time to worry.

Late on Friday afternoon as Mama was in the usual last minute rush to get the Sabbath meal ready, the telephone rang. Mama answered. As Becky listened, prickles of fear traveled up and down her spine. But Mama's voice was calm enough.

"No, Mimi, you can't sleep over at Barbara's tonight. It's *shabbos*."

Pause.

"Of course she's a nice girl and her mother will be there the whole time, but you know better. On Friday night we are one family here at home. You can stay with Barbara some other time."

Becky knew without any doubt now that Mimi had done it after all. Poor Mama, poor Papa! What a shock it would be for them! She offered to help Mama get dinner ready, polish the candlesticks, sweep the floor, do anything at all to help, as though this would make up in advance for the bad news that would soon come. Mama, poor innocent Mama, was delighted with Becky's sudden domesticity and even Papa remarked about it.

"Well, Becky, I never knew you were such a little homemaker. Of Mimi I was sure and there's no question about Dori. But you? It just goes to show, you never know your own daughters!"

Becky winced. He'd find out about his daughters soon enough. Becky worried for him, as though she were the mother and he were the child. Now, as he washed, he sang a little song he liked, a song without words—"Ay, tum, tum diddy, dum, dum, dum"—a little out of tune and faintly recognizable. And Mama—busy in the kitchen, stirring the soup and stopping to cut the lemon for the fish now browning in the oven, looked as tidy in her apron and as innocent as a little mother hen.

Thank heaven, there would be no company that night, no lonely cousins, no stray relatives, no poor soul with no other place to go.

"Where's Mimi?" Papa asked as they sat down at the table. Dori was spinning a long drawn out story for him and Papa was not yet impatient. Yet it was past the time to lift the silver wine cup and make the blessing.

"She'll be here in a minute," Mama said. "She's late, but she did telephone a while ago."

When Dori finished her story, Becky in an effort to distract her father began to tell him about the track meet. But when Papa looked at his watch again and Mimi was still absent, he became annoyed.

"All right, I'll telephone this Barbara Bentley, whoever she is. You know how girls are," Mama said, trying to calm Papa. "They talk and talk and talk and there's still something more to say. I know. I was the same way when I was a girl."

She pushed back her chair and at that very moment Mimi came in through the kitchen door. She went to her bedroom, threw her coat on the bed, and stood there, hesitating.

"Well?" Papa called out so she could hear. "How long do we wait now?"

A minute later Mimi slipped into her chair. Her cheeks glowed with an unnatural brightness; she wore a wide false smile; and she had tied a gaudy flowered scarf around her head like a turban.

"Where did you get such a kerchief and why do you wear it in the house? You can take it off, Mimi," Mama said, plainly puzzled.

"But don't you think it's pretty? It's a new look. Barbara let me borrow it," Mimi's voice was as high and unnatural as her smile.

"You heard your mother. Take off that rag," Papa said, close to the end of his patience.

Mimi moved her hands slowly, as though they were automatons and could go no faster. Everybody watched and waited. Dori's mouth hung open and Becky was biting her nails. Mimi felt as though she were in the middle of the stage with a spotlight on her and a thousand eyes watching. It took forever to untie the knot that held the kerchief, but at last it came undone. As she took the scarf away, her hair tumbled down.

Mama clapped her hand over her mouth to stop the scream that wanted to come out. Papa's face turned deathly white. Becky closed her eyes, not daring to look any more, and Dori gave a loud shocked gasp.

Mimi's hair had become a nightmare of white, yellowish and green tangles with the black strands that had not taken the bleach showing through. Mimi's smile grew wider and more painful than ever.

"It's a surprise," she said in a tiny weak voice.

"Who did this thing to you? What . . . I don't understand . . . is this some sort of joke? What is this?" Papa roared. They had seen him angry before, but never like this.

Tears that would not be blinked back flooded Mimi's eyes. The false smile changed to a howl and finally uncontrollable sobs racked her whole body. She ran to the bedroom, slammed the door, and threw herself on the bed where she sobbed hysterically.

Papa was as puzzled as he was enraged. He turned to Becky for an explanation.

"She wanted to be a blonde, so she had her hair bleached."

"She wants *blonde* hair? Why, in the name of heaven, *why?* She wants a good spanking, that's what she really wants. Such craziness!" Papa was more astonished than angry. But for all his talk of spanking, nobody worried that he would be doing any of it. What little spanking had to be done was always left to Mama who could not do it either.

"I don't understand," Papa said, looking defeated and baffled. "What girl ever had more beautiful black hair? How could she do such a thing?"

Becky, on the verge of tears herself, explained that it was Barbara Bentley who kept urging her on and that it wasn't really Mimi's fault, and then there had been the bet, so it was Becky's fault too in a way. All the while the sobs from the bedroom grew louder.

"I'll teach her to dye her hair. I'll teach her to dress up like that," Papa threatened, his anger rising again, but he still looked stunned, as though he could not believe what he had just seen.

"Listen, Danny," Mama said in a soothing voice. "She's punished enough, poor girl. Listen to her. Besides, it's Sabbath; this is no time to get angry. Wait a little. I'll go and talk with her."

Mama went to the bedroom while everyone else waited. The sobs grew weaker and weaker and finally stopped altogether. Mama returned to the dining room while Mimi went to wash her face.

"Now remember, don't stare at her and don't talk about it," Mama whispered. "Pretend it never happened."

It wasn't easy. Never had a Sabbath been more strained. Papa mumbled the blessing and did not say another word. Dori tried to break the deadly silence, for nobody could think of anything to say in this family that ordinarily found it hard to keep quiet, but all she could think of was a sweet strained remark that passed unanswered.

"I think I saw a robin today. Do you think that's a sign of spring? Huh, do you think so?"

Mama asked Becky how the track meet had come off, forgetting that Becky had already told her father about it, but Becky answered anyway. All their voices seemed as high and light and false as Dori's. From time to time Becky's eyes were drawn to Mimi's hair as though she were hypnotized, and each glance made her heart sink lower. It was awful, unbelievably awful.

"And I'll have to give her my locket too," she remembered.

All in all, it was a terrible evening and everyone was grateful when at last it was time to go to bed.

"Thank heavens for Mrs. Kirby!" Mama said and all three daughters agreed. Mrs. Kirby on the third floor was a hairdresser and one of Mama's staunchest admirers since Mama had nursed her through a long bout of pneumonia the year before.

On Saturday morning Mama, Becky, and Mimi went up to see her.

"Oh my dear, oh my dear child!" Mrs. Kirby gasped when she saw Mimi. "Who has done this awful thing to you? Oh, child, your bee-yoo-ti-ful black hair! Oh my, oh my!"

Mrs. Kirby's air of tragedy made Mimi even more forlorn looking, if that were possible. She stood in the middle of Mrs. Kirby's kitchen while Mrs. Kirby walked around her muttering, "Tsk-tsk, how could anyone *do* such a terrible thing!"

Mrs. Golden could have wept at the pale drawn look of her daughter, and Becky tried to smile encouragement while Mrs. Kirby carried on. Perhaps it had been a mistake to go to her. Mrs. Kirby had neither daughters nor sons nor the thick black hair with which all the Goldens were blessed, and it took her a little while to get over what she considered a criminal assault. But once the first shock was over, she became very professional and Mimi took hope.

"The first thing, Mimi, is not to worry. It's not a permanent condition. You'll get over it in time. But I'm afraid we'll have to use the scissors so that it will grow in blacker more quickly."

"How short will it be? As short as Becky's?" Mimi gulped, for the short boyish cap of black curls that seemed so right for Becky would be more than Mimi could endure on herself.

"No, dearie, just down to your shoulders, or a trifle shorter. It's more fashionable anyway. Your hair will grow in again, don't worry. Good hair grows fast. Well, shall we begin?"

Mimi sat down gingerly on the kitchen chair Mrs. Kirby set in the middle of the kitchen. She wrapped a large towel around Mimi and took out her comb and scissors. As the locks of hair fell to the floor, Mimi shut her eyes in agony and Mama tried to encourage her with brave smiles and remarks about how it was looking better already.

Mrs. Kirby spent the rest of the morning washing Mimi's hair and exclaiming with triumphant "there, there's" every time a bit of the dye came out. She brushed, patted, coaxed, and fussed over Mimi's hair until she could do no more with it.

"It's not so bad," Becky said weakly. She thought Mimi looked as if she had striped hair.

"There now, it will come in blacker and thicker than ever," Mrs. Kirby promised, "but don't you ever let it happen again."

"As if I would," Mimi said.

Mama wanted to pay Mrs. Kirby for her morning's work, but Mrs. Kirby wouldn't hear of it. "It's such a privilege to do something for you, Mrs. Golden, when you've done so much for me. When I think of that time you helped me through the pneumonia and the way you helped us out when my Tom was out of work, I know you're an angel and I could never do enough for you."

"Well, maybe not an angel," Mrs. Golden said, embarrassed by Mrs. Kirby's extravagant praise, "but perhaps you'd accept a *challeh?* Becky, run downstairs and bring one up. Fortunately I made two of them yesterday."

"Now that's real nice," Mrs. Kirby said and in another minute she was holding one of Mama's breads. "The way you braid bread, Mrs. Golden, I think you'd be a marvel with hair!"

Mama promised to send up more bread next week and Mimi, relieved that the worst was over, hugged Mrs. Kirby in gratitude. The venture had been painful, but it was far from being a tragedy.

Mimi could hardly tear herself away from the mirror. She could not explain whether she was attracted or repelled by the strange image that was her, and yet not her at all.

"What's funny," she told Becky, "is that I never liked me before. I always wanted to look like someone else, even before Barbara Bentley came along. Now I can't wait to look like myself again."

"You're you. You always will be," Becky said, "so don't worry."

She took the gold locket from its box and looked at it tenderly. It was a dull gold in an old fashioned oval shape, pretty enough and yet it was not its prettiness but its special meaning that made it valuable. It was an object that tied her to her family of another place at another time, a link between her and those few people who were left behind and yet were somehow part of it. Now that she was about to give up her locket, she understood what made it so valuable.

"Here, Mimi," she said, holding it out to her, "it's yours."

"Oh no, Becky, I don't want it. I couldn't take it. Anyway, my hair's not all bleached, only about half of it, so I didn't win. Nor did you."

"If you really feel that way . . . well, thanks, Mimi," Becky said softly. Now she put the locket around her neck and was glad to feel it there. The locket was more than a pretty ornament to her now.

A few seconds later she heard Mimi talking, more to herself than to Becky. "I never want to see Barbara Bentley again. Not ever."

"It's about time," Becky said.

But Mimi knew Becky didn't understand and she wasn't about to explain. Mimi forgave Barbara for the unfortunate bleaching; it couldn't have been easy to manage all of Mimi's hair. But she could not forgive Barbara for looking down on Mama and Mrs. Wilensky because of their accent. Mimi felt a burning shame for not having defended Mama. The short striped hair was a penance that she almost welcomed.

8

Becky and Lisa

They were the best of friends and they walked home from school together almost every day. Becky never understood quite why, yet they were friends anyway. Lisa liked to talk about boys and Becky liked to talk about horses. As Lisa began first that day and chatted on—"Eric is cuter than Marty, isn't he, but Marty's a perfect dancer; and yet I kinda like Carl"—talk that could go on for hours, Becky was thinking that her father had looked worried that morning. Yesterday another letter had come from Bernard.

"The one I really like is Roland, but he won't even look at me."

Becky wondered how she could like Lisa so much when she suddenly felt so exasperated with her. Fortunately they were passing by Lasker's. It was Wednesday, the day when the fresh pickles came; the odor drifted out as a customer opened the door.

"Hey, let's get a pickle!" Becky cried.

"Sure. Let's!"

However different the girls might be, they agreed on at least one matter. Pickles. Mrs. Lasker picked long green dills from the salty brine, put a protective paper around each, and accepted a nickel apiece from the girls. At least, Becky thought, Lisa was too busy with the pickle to talk about boys.

"You're awfully quiet today," Lisa said. "I haven't heard

you mention horses at all. Anything wrong?"

"No, not really. I was just thinking about my father. He gets so sad when he hears from his cousin in Austria. Do you have any relatives over there?"

"Sure. My father says every Jew, well almost every one, has someone over there. He has a sister and if only he could get enough money, he'd send for her. Then he curses the Depression and being put out of work all the time. It's really awful there."

"Do they talk about it a lot at your house?" Becky asked.

"In a way. My brother and my father keep following the news, over the radio and in the papers, and my mother can't stand it. She says there's going to be another war. But even when they don't talk about it, somehow it's there."

"I know," Becky said. "You can't get away from it. I think my parents don't like to talk about it too much in front of us—that is, I hear them talking in low voices a lot after we go to bed—and I guess parents want to keep their kids from getting too frightened and worried. But even when we talk about other things, it's still there, like something in the air. I can't explain it. It's sort of heavy."

"It's like that at our house too, sometimes. Other times, you'd never know anything was wrong, and then you turn on the radio, and there it is. We're lucky to be here in this country."

"We sure are," Becky said, and yet she felt guilty. It was only luck that she was born here and not in Europe. "I think we ought to do something to help, because we are lucky. But I don't know what."

"Don't worry, Becky. That's what my mother tells me. Don't worry, because you can't do anything about it. The best thing you can do, my mother says, is make your own life good. So mine is good, I guess. Anyway, let's not talk about it. Tell me something, Becky, do you think Arnold likes me? You know, Arnold with the striped sweater?"

So the conversation was back to boys again. No wonder either, Lisa was pretty; even when she sucked her pickles she was pretty. And Becky thought it was very odd that her best friend should be so concerned with boys and pretty clothes and ballet lessons, when all she cared about—her mind fluttered to find the exact words and came up with the vision of a palomino prancing through a fresh green meadow and kicking up his heels in the excitement of another spring.

"Becky, you aren't even listening to me."

"I was too."

"What did I say?"

"Something about Robert Wise. He's big."

Lisa laughed. "Oh Becky, you're funny. I know you. You were thinking about some horse. You know, you're really crazy. I'll bet you've never even been on a horse."

"I certainly have. I can prove it."

"You were on a horse? Becky Golden, that's an f-i-b!"

Becky's eyes blazed. "Come up to my house. Right now. I'll show you a photograph. I was seven years old and this man came around to take pictures of kids sitting on his pony. Boy, I remember it as clear. . . ." She took a last bite of pickle and sighed.

"You weren't living here then, Lisa. The man who came around might have been a gypsy, you know, because he was dark with a gold tooth in front. At least I thought of him as a gypsy. He had a camera on his back and he was leading a white pony with brown patches, so I followed him all the way down the street."

"That I do believe."

"He kept saying, 'Hey kid, get lost!' out of the side of his mouth. He had to talk that way because he had a cigarette dangling from his lips."

Becky paused to imitate him and then continued.

"He knocked on every door and told the mothers he would take a picture of their kids on the pony. That poor man! He had more doors slammed in his face. Nobody had any money and to think of spending what little they had for a picture of their child on a pony—that poor man was so discouraged."

"So what happened?" When Becky talked she acted and Lisa could practically see the man and a small excited Becky reaching up to touch the pony.

"When he came to our house, and of course I was following him every bit of the way, my mother came to the door. She was going to say no like the others. She said she would like a picture of me but why on a horse? It didn't make sense. Well, I went to her and pulled at her skirt, looked up at her and begged. It was the first time in my life I begged for anything, 'Please, Mama, just this once, please.' So she asked, 'How much is it?'

" 'T'irty-five cents. See, ma'am, we put de pitcher on a board like dis and it will come in the mail two weeks, t'ree weeks, somet'in' like dat. You don't need to worry. You'll get it.'

"Well, thirty-five cents was a lot of money. The Depression was much worse then than it is now and my father really had a hard time getting work. There were lots of men just hanging around Hope Street because they couldn't find any jobs. But my mother thought, 'I'm kissing this money good-by and I'll never see it again, but if it makes Becky happy, it's worth it.' At least that's what I imagine she said."

"Sounds like her. I love your mother," Lisa said.

"But wait! She told the man he had to give me a ride to the end of the street and back first, because she knew I was crazy about horses, and then he could take my picture. He grumbled but he did it and she paid him. I never felt so wonderful in all my life as I did then. All the kids were

looking at me. I remember one other thing. Mama told him
to wait a minute and then she made a sandwich for him
because she thought he looked hungry. I followed him some
more and then I had to go home. He must have been
relieved when I did.

"Well, we waited and waited and the picture didn't
come. Then when we gave up and my father told my
mother she'd been taken, the picture came. My father loved
it and made a frame for it."

By this time the girls had come to Becky's house and
Becky took Lisa into the living room where the photograph
hung. Becky remembered what her father had said when he
first saw it, but she didn't want to tell Lisa because it
sounded so egotistical, but she would never forget.

"Beautiful, Becky, beautiful! She sits there like a princess!"

He had looked at Becky with eyes of love and admiration
and she had brimmed over with pride and happiness. It was
from that time on that horses came to her in daydreams and
at night, when she was scolded or when school was boring
or when Papa was out of work and a cloud of despair hung
over the house. And when Dori was tiny and Papa held her
on his lap and hardly noticed Becky anymore, the horse had
come for her then too.

"Lisa," she said, "I'm going to tell you a secret. Promise
not to tell?"

Lisa promised.

"I'm going to get a real horse."

"Becky, you're crazy. A real horse on Hope Street?"

Becky did not smile. "I can't tell you the details, not now.
But a real horse is going to come. You wait and see. I know
this. It's a fact."

Lisa sighed for her friend, but Becky knew she was right.
Some day a real horse would come.

9

Action!

Becky sat at the scarred wooden desk in her math class and it was clear that she was thinking intensely. Miss Robertson approved; so few of her students ever seemed to think. But Miss Robertson could not know that the arithmetic problem she had just written on the blackboard was not the problem Becky was wrestling with. Becky's problem was very private, a problem about the nature of wishes.

Mimi's wish had come true and hers hadn't. Why? She wasn't jealous, considering what had happened, but she was trying to analyze why it had worked for Mimi and not for her. That Mimi's wish backfired and at the time seemed a catastrophe was beside the point. A week later it seemed like the catastrophe may well have been a blessing in its own way. Mimi was no longer the silly little copycat trailing after Barbara Bentley, but seemed to have emerged into a new Mimi, calmer than she'd ever been. Only the night before she had confessed to Becky: "It's not that I think a lot of myself or anything like that, but I'm glad enough to be me. I'd never thought of it before."

Becky thought what happened to Mimi was like those fairy tales in which a person is granted three wishes, but something always happens to foil them so that they're not what they seem.

What bothered Becky was that Mimi's wish had been

such a foolish one, trying to be someone else. It invited failure. But it seemed so right for Becky to have a horse. She had dreamed about them so long. Did some mysterious power decide which wishes would be granted? How did it work?

"Yes, Becky, I can tell you've been thinking hard. What's the answer?" Miss Robertson asked hopefully.

Becky, startled to find herself in class once more, looked up and in that instant the answer to her problem leaped into her head. And like most answers it was simplicity itself. Mimi's wish had come true because Mimi had not sat about waiting, but had done something about making it happen.

And as she looked at Miss Robertson, Becky remembered those quotations her teacher had repeated so many times. "Where there's a will there's a way," and "Heaven helps those who help themselves!" Of course, that was the answer!

"Well, Becky, we're waiting," Miss Robertson said, not so patiently this time.

Becky blinked, looked up at the problem on the board and tried to figure it out, but all around her hands flew up in the air and Miss Robertson, disappointed in her star pupil, had to turn to someone else.

No wonder the horse wouldn't come, she thought. What did she really know about horses? True, she had read every book about them that the library could offer; she studied them in the westerns she saw at the Bijou every Saturday afternoon; and she collected pictures of horses. But excepting for her one experience in riding a pony, she had never even been close to a horse.

Where could she find horses? In a stable. Of course. The inspiration was too great to be believed; she could work in a stable after school and learn about horses, and with the money she made, she would save to buy her own horse. Now she was on her way at last!

She ran home from school, not even waiting for Lisa who was talking to Carl or Eric or Marty, and without even stopping to talk with Mama, pulled out the telephone book and looked up STABLES in the yellow pages. Eight stables were listed, which meant eight chances. But when Becky looked at the addresses, she found that most of them were outside the city limits and she would have no way of getting there. There was one that wasn't too impossible, McMurdie's Happy Horse Stable located in Victoria Park. It was not too close to home and there'd be the matter of bus fare, but if she rode one way and walked the other, it might not be too difficult.

She had better not tell Mama, she thought, at least not until she had a job. Mama wanted the girls to stay around home or at least within a certain radius. Outside, she had said, it could be dangerous, although she never explained why. "Home is safe," was all she would say.

"But I can't stay here forever," Becky thought as she put on the brown corduroy pants that were handed down from her cousin, Sam. She put on her jacket and baseball cap, took two cookies from the jar, and went to the door.

"I'm going out for a little while, Mama," she said.

Mama, frowning over a complicated gathering she was making in a skirt, looked up briefly, assumed she was going to Lisa's, and said absently, "All right, darling, be home before it's dark."

Becky cried, "Good-by," and although her mother was suggesting that she wear a sweater because it wasn't too warm outside, she didn't hear, because she was rushing down the stairs and flying to catch the bus that went near Victoria Park.

The signs pointing to the Happy Horse Stable led Becky

along a curving road to the back of a pine grove where two long rows of stables delighted her by looking exactly like the stables she had seen in picture books. A girl in a brown riding habit complete with cap and boots was mounting a handsome chestnut horse. Becky stopped in awe as the horse walked with dignity to the riding path of red gravel that led through the woods and soon disappeared from her view.

"Someday that will be me," Becky thought to herself.

At the end of the stables lay an open field bounded by a circle of rail fences where Becky caught glimpses of a girl who was probably not much older than herself trotting around on a—

A big sigh escaped her. To think that all this was not so very far from her home and she hadn't known about it before. If she could work in this loveliest of places, she would be so grateful, she would never again complain about anything. This was a place where she could live forever and never wish to leave.

Excited and timid at the same time, for she had never before asked for work, she knocked on the office door, but nobody answered. She walked along the path that led to the stables while the horses in their stalls looked at her. How aristocratic they are, she thought, and how big! She longed to pet them, but didn't dare, afraid they might bite.

A tall man with stringy red hair that escaped from a plaid cap emerged from a distant stall and walked up the aisle, pails in either hand. As he looked at Becky questioningly, she asked in a voice that was suddenly very tiny and high, "Pardon me, but I'm looking for Mr. McMurdy."

"Yes, I'm Mr. McMurdy, and what is it you're wanting?"

He seemed somewhat harrassed, as though he were in a hurry. Becky spoke as quickly as she could.

"I was wondering if you needed someone to help every

day in the stables. After school, I mean. I could curry the horses and clean the stalls and feed the horses . . . well, whatever you wanted to have done."

"H'm," Mr. McMurdy put down the pails and scratched his head so that the plaid cap was pushed way back and came perilously close to falling off. "I do need help, that's the truth. My last boy ran out on me, drat him, right when I needed him the most. You ever work aroun' horses before, lad?"

Becky wished he hadn't said "lad," but she answered his question truthfully. "No sir, but I could learn. I learn very fast."

"You look awfully skinny. Think you could handle it?"

"Oh yes, sir. I'm thin but I'm very strong. And I promise I'd never run off and leave you."

"You wouldn't, eh?" A ghost of a smile crossed Mr. McMurdy's face and he rubbed the stubble on his chin.

"I could come after school every day and work at least two hours. Saturday afternoons and part of Sunday too," she added.

"You're an eager one, aren't ya? I s'pose you like horses."

"Yes, sir! If you wanted me to exercise them, I could do that too. Once you showed me how, that is."

"Well, I do need help. You look awfully skinny, but I guess I can give you a try. Can you start tomorrow?"

"I sure could," Becky was grinning and her eyes were shining. It was all so much simpler than she had expected. Mr. McMurdy began to walk to the office and Becky followed. She'd have to remember to ask him how much he would pay her, for although she didn't like to talk about money, Mama had taught her that in any business everything must be understood clearly at the outset. She would settle for very little if it meant being near those horses.

"What's your name, lad?" Mr. McMurdy said, putting down his pails.

"Becky,"

"Huh? Becky!" Mr. McMurdy stopped short and looked at her closely. "What's your real name?" This time he did not say "lad."

"Rebecca Golden," Becky's voice had dropped very low.

"Oh my gawsh! Here I was thinking you was a boy. Look, girlie, I'm sorry as I can be, but I can't have no girl doin' that work."

"But Mr. McMurdy, I'm as strong as a boy. Honest. What difference would it make?"

"Well, there's lots of things to consider, y'know. Like you could hurt yerself carryin' the pails. Or you could get kicked by a horse. Sometimes they turn mean."

"But couldn't a boy get hurt if a horse kicked him? Wouldn't that be just as terrible?"

"Sure, it would be turrible, but not quite so turrible as if it happened to a gurrul. What would your father and mother do to me if you got kicked or bitten, eh?"

"It's not fair. Girls ride horses, like that one there."

"That's not the same thing. Y'see, they own those horses. It's their risk. Not the same thing at all. I'm sorry, Becky, you're a nice gurrul, but I can't hire no gurrul for that kind of work."

Becky looked at him with large green eyes full of disappointment.

"Sorry, lass," he said, "I can tell you really like the horses."

With that he picked up his pails and walked back to the stables. Becky looked after him and then cried to herself, "It's not fair, it's not!"

Then, because she had no more money for busfare, she walked all the way home and wondered again why the wish worked for Mimi and not for her.

10

A Happy Accident

"Becky, do you think you could go to the store for me? I need a loaf of rye bread. Mrs. Lieberman is coming for a fitting for a dress, her daughter's getting married, and anyway I can't go. Would you mind, Becky?"

Becky didn't mind. The Bartons, the family next door, were having another bitter fight which happened when Mr. Barton came home drunk, and Becky hated to listen to it. And she hadn't planned to go over to Lisa's because Lisa had another of her endless ballet lessons, so she said to her mother, "Sure, I don't mind."

"I'm so lucky in my daughters," Mama had said more than once, "because they are all different." It was true. Becky, the restless one, ran the errands and sometimes delivered dresses to customers. Mimi helped with the cooking when Mama was too busy and she knew how to decorate cakes as well. And Dori was already clever enough at sewing to help Mama with the basting and finishing of the seams.

"And while you're at it, Becky, I need a box of oatmeal, a bar of laundry soap, and if it's not too much to carry, a can of tomato soup and a pound of onions."

"That sure is dull," Becky pouted. "Why can't you need things like pickles or halvah or black olives?" Becky's passion for pickles was exceeded only by her love for black olives. If only they weren't so expensive!

"All right, darling. Get yourself a pickle. One pickle, just for you. And tell Mr. Lasker to charge it. Can you remember everything? Want to write it down?"

"No." Becky scorned writing down lists. The doorbell rang and Mrs. Golden kissed Becky good-by on her way to welcome Mrs. Lieberman.

The only trouble with Lasker's store, Becky decided, was that one had to wait and wait and wait some more, because not only was the store full of customers but Mr. Lasker felt obliged to make little jokes for each customer, even someone who only came in for a box of matches, and Mrs. Lasker felt a social obligation to each of her clients.

It was always: "Hello, Mrs. Roth, and how is your baby feeling today? Did the new tooth come through?"

And then Becky would have to wait while Mrs. Roth described the emergence of Lennie's tooth and how it had been with Maxie when his teeth were coming through and how difficult it had been with Julie, her first.

At least Lasker's store had a fascination that other stores did not. Crocks and barrels of garlicky pickles and pickled herrings put out a pungent odor no other store could match. A new barrel of white sauerkraut dotted here and there with red cranberries had just been opened and Becky wished Mama had ordered some of it. Becky's eyes strayed to the back of the store where huge rounds of cheese and a high loaf of marbled halvah stood temptingly just out of reach. If only Becky were the one to choose the groceries, how different they would be.

Let's see, what did Mama want? Bread, oatmeal, a bar of laundry soap, a can of something. But what? Corn? Tomatoes? It didn't sound quite right. She let her eyes run from one shelf to another. Sooner or later she would recall what it was Mama wanted.

However, as she glanced from one shelf to another, over

and around the waiting customers, something stopped her so short that she completely forgot what she was looking for. This was the most important thing that had happened to her yet!

On the side of a box of cereal were slanting red letters:

YOU CAN WIN WONDER, THE WONDER HORSE!

It was followed by the silhouette of a horse running, his mane flying out behind him.

A contest! She stood there blinking with the wonder of it. Like the best solutions to most problems, it was so direct and simple she hadn't even thought of it. Becky's talent, if any, lay in winning contests. Unlike Mimi or Lisa who had never won anything at all, Becky never failed to win at least something in every contest she entered, even if it only turned out to be a cake of soap or a pen that didn't work too well. A treasury of winnings proved her good luck: the baseball cap with the blue visor, a kewpie doll, a silver whistle which no longer whistled and wasn't really silver, and any number of pens and pencils. Her best prize was a Donald Duck watch that ticked so loud it could be heard from one end of the house to the other. Unfortunately this irritated Papa who declared it an insult to the art of watchmaking. So Becky didn't wear it when he was around.

Nevertheless, Becky was a born winner of contests. And she was going to win WONDER. She looked at the box and a series of small waving chills traveled up and down her spine, because she *knew*, just as she always knew when she was about to win a prize, that this was meant for her.

Would Mama mind very much if she bought Bixie Cereal instead of oatmeal, just this once, for she was sure she would need at least one boxtop and maybe two. If she went without the pickle, that would be a saving of five cents. Contests were such silly things, she knew; most likely she would have to send in one or two boxtops and twenty-five words on why she loved Bixies. They probably tasted dreadful but she'd eat every last one of them if it meant winning WONDER.

And she was going to win Wonder. She knew it, she knew it without a doubt. Her heart was full of ecstasy, right there in Lasker's grocery.

"Yes, young lady, I suppose you're dreaming about your boyfriend. Or boy friends. Isn't that what young ladies are supposed to do?"

Becky gave him a sickly smile. Idiot, she thought. Yet she could not be angry with anyone on this very important day. She'd even listen to his dreadful jokes.

She told him everything that her mother wanted, finally remembering that the item she had forgotten was tomato soup. At the very last she asked almost breathlessly for a box of Bixies, please, and as soon as it was all totaled on the back of the brown paper bag and the groceries packed inside, Becky added, "Charge it, please," and ran out of the store while the waiting customers looked at her and then at each other. "What a hurry she's in!" one said. "It's a boyfriend, I think," Mr. Lasker added.

At home Becky read the rules of the contest even before she took off her coat. It was just as she expected. Two box tops and twenty-five words.

"Please, Mama, can I buy another box? I'll sweep the kitchen, carry out the garbage, anything at all. Please, Mama."

"It's not the price of the box, Becky. It's what we do, if, God forbid, you win the horse. What will you do with a horse? Where will you keep him? What will you feed him? Bixies?"

"Oh Mama, we can worry about that later."

"It says here," Mrs. Golden continued, "that instead of a

horse you can take two hundred and fifty dollars in cash. Second prize, a bicycle. Third prize, a tennis racquet. You won one of those already. Becky, if only you were interested in something sensible like tennis. I could make you a white tennis dress with a short swingy skirt."

While Mama dreamed of Becky flying over a tennis court, Becky was flying down the street to Lasker's for another box of Bixies.

The rest of that afternoon and all that evening after dinner, Becky sat at the kitchen table and she bit her pencil as she wondered what was the best way to make use of her twenty-five words. She had already written almost fifty statements about why she loved Bixies, fifty lies she told herself, but each one had a flaw. No writer ever worked harder to achieve perfection. By eleven o'clock when she should have been in bed, she was still writing. But by the next morning, the two boxtops and the twenty-five words were in the mail.

Now all she had to do was wait. The contest wouldn't close until the end of April, which was unthinkably far away. But Becky could afford to wait. She knew she was going to win WONDER, THE WONDER HORSE.

11

March 13, 1938

Becky ran up the stairs two at a time and bounded into the kitchen. Spring was coming in earnest, at least it seemed so on that day, and it was torture to sit in school all day.

"Mama, any mail for me?" she asked. "Has the mail come yet?"

The whirring of the sewing machine came to a stop and Mrs. Golden looked at her daughter with an expression Becky had seen more than once. It was called exasperation. Or sympathy. Or, most likely a mixture of both.

"Becky, every day you ask the same question and every day I give you the same answer. They don't choose the winners until the end of April. Maybe later. The only mail that came is bills. And advertisements."

"It's so hard to wait," Becky said. She threw herself into her father's Morris chair, one long leg sprawled out and the other hung over the arm of the chair.

"She thinks she'll come home one day and find the horse sitting in the living room, waiting for her," Mimi said. She looked like a housewifely maiden with her hair tied back with a blue ribbon and her skirt and sweater covered with a fresh white apron. She was rolling out cookies and cutting them in flower shapes as she talked.

Too restless to stay down for long, Becky walked over to

the baked cookies that were cooling on the rack and bit into the prettiest one she could find.

"You leave those cookies alone. They're for Drama Club. Mama, make her stop taking them!"

With a devilish grin, Becky snapped up two more cookies and settled back in the chair.

"Mimi, Becky, no fighting! You both know better."

The telephone rang and Becky leaped to answer it. It was a boy asking for Mimi. Mimi slouched in her chair, cradled the receiver in her hand, giggled prettily at frequent intervals, and practiced a new low tone of voice meant to be sensuous.

"She's disgusting, Mama," Becky said.

"No, not disgusting, Becky. She's a girl. She's only trying on new voices, the way she tries on new dresses, to see which ones fit," Mama answered philosophically, but Becky made a face at Mimi anyway.

Ever since the hair-bleaching episode, Mimi was intent on discovering herself, as she called it. And she thought quite possibly the Drama Club was a good place to begin. She discovered that the scarves and ribbons and turbans she wore to hide the bleach marks in her hair "created a dramatic effect," as she told Mama. Mama now had to suffer long conferences with her about her wardrobe; Mimi wanted dresses that were lower here in front or darted there, and she wanted to try new colors such as "jealousy green" or "kiss-cherry red." "What kind of colors are they?" Mama had asked in alarm, but when she saw samples she nodded. "Green and red, that's all."

Mimi's manner of speaking was changing too. "Pure diction," she had described her new clipped speech. But she also adopted so many new styles that she might have been six different individuals. At the moment she was flirting with a seventh individual, a siren, and her facial gestures and artificial laugh were too much for Becky, who imitated her, picking up her mannerisms to an insulting degree. Mimi alternated between a giddy flirtation over the phone and furious glances at Becky.

Mama paid no attention and Becky could tell it wasn't one of her best days, as she picked up a razor and ripped out a seam. The windows were open and the radio from the next house blared into the kitchen, loud but not clear, only a noise punctuated with static.

"Mama, I'm going to the library," Becky said.

"You were there yesterday," Mama remarked. But Becky only sighed; she couldn't bear to stay in the house any longer, and the library was her refuge.

As she walked down the street, she found herself longing to be out somewhere in the country. She wasn't sure what the country looked like, for the Goldens had no car and most frequently stayed home. Becky had not minded too much, but now for the first time in her life, she wanted to escape Hope Street. Certainly she did not think of it as a slum, as did Mimi and Lisa Kline, but she was tired of its broken dirty sidewalks, the ailing houses with their ugly graffiti, and the endless bits of trash and newspapers that blew across the unswept street. She walked to the library and dreamed of open green fields, flocks of sheep with their new born lambs, and a pasture of horses frisking about in the new spring air.

As she was about to walk into the library, she practically bumped into her friend, Eileen Dolan.

Becky admired Eileen greatly, not only because of her long auburn braids and apple red cheeks, but because she had a space between her two front teeth through which she could whistle.

That afternoon she was particularly impressive in a green Girl Scout uniform, complete from the brimmed hat down to the emblemed socks. Bright round merit badges were sewn on her sleeves and on a sash that crossed in front. From a green webbed belt hung an array of equipment: a jack-knife, a silver whistle, compass, leather coin purse, and too many other items for Becky to take in at once, but all of them were marked with the Girl Scout emblem.

"That's some uniform!" Becky said in obvious admiration. "What are all those badges for? You must be awfully good to have all these."

Patiently Eileen explained them. This one was for first class, that one for special honors, this was a troop badge, and the merit badges were for laundry, camping, astronomy, observor, gardening, bee keeping. . . ."

"You mean you keep bees around here?" Becky interrupted.

"I do. I had a little hive out of a box. It wasn't too big. And I raised bees. Only they died after I got my merit badge."

"Can you get a merit badge for riding horses?"

"Sure, it's a lovely one. Our leader, Doxie, knows all about horses. You have to know how to take care of them and how to ride and stuff." Eileen could see Becky's eyes growing wide. "You should have joined the troop, Becky. You could still join, if you wanted."

Becky hesitated and her eyes fell. It was so hard to explain to Eileen. In Russia Mama had never heard of such things. She had been brought up to believe it was best to stay close to home, and although she knew it was different in this country, still she thought that the Girl Scouts and other organizations like it were too far from Hope Street.

"Look, Becky, we're having a survival hike this Saturday and you could come on that and see if you like it. And you

can meet Doxie and the girls. Oh please come, Becky. Say
you'll come."

"What's a survival hike?"

"We pretend we're in a place where we have to survive.
We hike for miles and we have to read maps and cook our
dinner. That's another thing. Just bring along an egg and an
orange for lunch."

"That's for lunch? That's all?"

"Yes, that's all! Doxie is so much fun. She says it's a
problem. If we're lost in the woods with an egg and orange,
how do we manage?"

It seemed absurd to Becky to think of being lost in the
woods with an egg and an orange. No wonder Mama had
hesitated about letting her join if that's what they did. But
then again, it was a way of getting to the country, and
maybe Doxie would talk to her about horses.

"Do I have to wear a uniform?" she asked.

"No. Just old pants and a sweater. Please come, Becky.
You'll love it." Eileen's voice rose high in a happy squeal.

Becky tried to imagine herself in a green uniform covered
with badges and knives and compasses dangling from the
belt, but somehow she couldn't see it. Still, she could
envision herself hiking over the hills.

"Okay," she said to Eileen. "If my mother lets me go, I'll
call you."

Eileen's face lit up with a happy smile. "You'll be glad if
you do. And I'll be glad too. So long now, Becky."

And with that she bounded away.

It was almost dark when Becky got home. She thought
there seemed to be some excitement in the streets, a feeling
of people hurrying faster than usual, but she could not
explain it.

When she walked in the kitchen, she saw her mother and

Lisa Kline's mother and Mrs. Goldstein who had come up from the first floor, and looking at their faces, wondering why they would be together so close to dinnertime, she knew something was wrong, very wrong.

"What's happened?" she cried, fearing the worst.

"Hitler has taken over Austria. The troops marched into Vienna today. So now Austria is part of Germany."

"And Cousin Bernard?" Becky asked.

"We don't know about him. About anyone. There were many Nazis in Austria and now. . . ."

"What they will do in Austria we don't know, but it's not hard to guess. It will be like Germany, maybe worse," Mrs. Kline said.

"I have relatives there too," Mrs. Goldstein said, "and they had said it couldn't happen. But now it's happening. Those poor people. I can hardly bear to think of it."

The three women became silent, as though there were nothing more they could say, and Becky felt the tragedy of it. Her fingers touched her grandmother's locket that she now wore all the time, and it reminded her that she was linked to all those innocent people whose future had suddenly become so grim.

12

Survival Hike

Either Eileen Dolan was the most enthusiastic girl Becky had ever known or the sudden turn in the weather, making Saturday bleak and wintery, was affecting her, because she was jumping up and down and rubbing her arms as she waited on the corner for Becky.

"So your mother let you come after all! Wonderful!"

"Yeah. But she thinks it's going to snow and she insisted I wear all this junk," Becky said in a muffled voice, ashamed to be so heavily protected in polo shirt, blouse, two sweaters, a jacket, a long woolen scarf, and a crocheted skating cap that was too big and kept falling down over her face.

"My mom is just as bad," Eileen consoled her. "But that's how moms are!"

"Sure, I don't really care," Becky said and wondered why she felt she had to lie about it.

Eileen would never know what a feat it was for Becky to get her mother to let her take this hike. And at the last minute she really didn't want to go but was too ashamed to back out.

"A survival hike! Why do the Girl Scouts have to worry about survival? They're nice American girls. They're not in Europe fleeing from the Nazis. I don't understand, Becky." Mama was never sarcastic; she meant it. To someone who had really faced the problem of survival, pretended survival was beyond her understanding.

"Oh Mama, it's just something that they do. And they asked me to go with them. We'll be walking in the country."

"They'll ask you again when the weather is nicer. I think it's going to snow."

"Mama, it's *March*. It won't snow."

"The Girl Scouts promise you it won't snow? So tell me, who has told them that they can be so sure? That they can make such promises?" Mama shook her head as if to ask, "You really expect me to believe that?" But when she saw how much Becky wanted to go, she softened. "All right, Becky, you can go. But you'd better take carfare. It's too long to hike to Bloomfield."

"You don't understand, Mama. It's a *survival* hike. It's supposed to prove how strong you are. Only sissies would take a bus."

Mama could not understand about the orange and egg either. "Better take along a peanut butter sandwich too. Just in case you get hungry."

Becky looked at her aghast. "But Mama, that would be cheating."

"Becky, who can survive on an orange and an egg? A peanut butter sandwich is cheating, when your life is in danger? This doesn't make sense."

Becky slumped in the kitchen chair. Mama's voice changed.

"Poor Becky, it can't be much fun around here. The radio broadcasts, the newspapers, such awful news. It's hard to be cheerful with all that's going on. And you're still a child. This hike sounds crazy, but maybe you should go, get out in the country, be with other girls. But Becky, you take with you a peanut butter sandwich."

Becky could tell Mama was going to give her a hard time

about that peanut butter sandwich, so she took it without a word, but she had no intention of letting anyone see her with it. After kissing Mama good-by, she skipped down the stairs and thought of leaving it on the cellar steps, but if Mama found it, she would be hurt. So she took it with her. On the way to the corner where she was to meet Eileen, she passed a mailbox. The perfect solution! She dropped it inside, an anonymous contribution. And nobody, excepting a puzzled mailman, would ever know.

One by one the girls showed up and Eileen introduced her to each of them. They all went to the school Eileen now attended and Becky was shy about meeting so many new girls. How would she ever remember their names? But before she could speak with any of them, they began to jump up and down. "Doxie's coming!"

Becky had to agree that this tall, sandy-haired Doxie was an impressive young woman. Something about her, perhaps the long jaw and the protruding teeth, reminded Becky of a horse. Much as she loved horses, however, she did not think she would care to look like one.

Becky much preferred Gaby, a small brown-eyed girl of eighteen or so. Her eyes reminded her of those of a tiny woodland animal.

"Hey, Doxie," one of the girls cried, "my mother says it's going to snow and we ought to postpone the hike."

"Mine did too."

"What d'you know? So did mine."

"Mine said it's awful to survive on a cold day like this and you have to survive when it's warm too, so let's wait until it's warm."

Becky was shivering and hoped that in the light of all this protest Doxie would call the hike off. Then she could go to the movies with Lisa that afternoon or stay for the meeting of Mimi's Drama Club. But Doxie was of sterner stuff. She faced the group squarely, reminding Becky of the army sergeants that appeared in war movies.

"So this is my top scouting unit! Summer soldiers, afraid of a little chill. All right, any little sugar bun can run home to Mama, but the real scouts will forge on ahead. Now then, who are my scouts?"

"I am, Doxie."

"Me, too."

Becky wouldn't have minded being a sugar bun and going home, but it might embarrass Eileen. And Mimi would laugh at her.

And so the hike began and Becky kept up as well as she could. Doxie was in front and set the pace with long loping strides. Bit by bit Becky fell behind until she was at the end of the group. The muscles in the back of her legs were aching and they hadn't even reached the edge of the city.

It wouldn't be so bad if only there were someone to talk with. The girls were polite and one or two of them were friendly enough, but they knew each other and talked about people and events Becky had not heard of. Whenever a bus passed, Becky looked at it longingly. Mama had been right after all.

"Are you all right, Becky?" Gaby had stepped beside her and asked in a quiet voice so the others wouldn't hear.

"Oh yes, I'm fine," Becky whispered back. She attempted a wide smile.

Gaby grinned back as if she understood. "Good for you! Doxie rushes it too much for new girls, but you'll do all right."

She smiled encouragingly and moved up front with Doxie.

"Let's SING!" Doxie shouted. "Pass it along." It was an order. The girls passed it along dutifully.

She would have enjoyed singing if only her feet didn't ache so much. They sang marching songs, folk songs, and many silly songs imitating animals which Dori would have loved. The voices grew weaker, however, and soon the singing stopped.

"We'll fall out for a rest in another mile or so!" Doxie called out cheerfully. A mile! "I'll die before I get there!" Becky groaned. She was sure Doxie could survive anything anywhere. But Becky trudged on and at last Doxie stopped.

"Here's the plan," she said, talking out of the side of her mouth as though it were highly confidential information. "Pretend we're in a stress situation, a war or earthquake, anything you like. We all have to meet at a certain place but we can't travel together. There are three different routes; we'll divide into three groups, each with its own map; and we'll meet at the Reid Chalet and have lunch. OK?"

Becky remembered what Mama said. Everybody could laugh and joke and play at disaster because they just didn't believe it could ever really happen. And yet . . . she touched the gold locket under her shirt. How many poor people were there in Europe now, relatives, Jews—and gypsies too, she had heard—who were struggling through the snows wondering if they could survive and knowing there was the real possibility that they wouldn't?

Before she could rest her tired legs, Freckles, the leader of the group Becky was in, studied the map and then blew her whistle.

"C'mon, you guys. Let's get a good start and not come in last."

Eileen who was in another group turned to wave good-by to Becky as she took off. And Gaby whispered "Good luck!" in a quiet voice as she walked by. Becky had no choice but to follow Freckles.

Holding a map in her hand, Freckles scrambled over a

stone wall and attempted to stride over the frozen fields. Becky stumbled over the uneven turf, never having realized how hard it was to walk on. She followed the others, climbing under a barbed wire fence, following a dirt road that twisted and curved and then, after the girls disagreed with each other briefly, broke a path through woods thick with brush. It was sharp and the twigs that snapped off hurt. In the meanwhile, it began to snow large moist flakes.

"What more can happen!" Becky cried, exhausted. But the new horror was a railroad bridge and an argument arose as to whether they had to cross it or not. Freckles insisted they had no choice.

"But what if a train should come?" a frightened girl asked.

"Then we jump off," Freckles answered calmly.

"B-b-but there's a river down there. We'll drown," the girl complained and Freckles looked at her scathingly.

"You can swim, can't you?" she said scornfully.

The girls crossed the bridge in single file. Halfway across Becky looked down and found herself growing dizzy. She thought she heard a train whistle. Was it possible that it would come and that she could die here in the woods on a Girl Scout hike? "Please God, not yet," she prayed. "Not before I get my horse," she added. And this gave her courage. She looked ahead resolutely and walked across steadily. Once on the other side, she would have gladly kissed the solid ground, but she restrained herself in front of Freckles.

From that point on, the hike through the woods was less harrowing but seemed endless. The landscape was deserted except for a farmer they passed who was leading a cow through a frozen field. Becky, trailing behind and aching with weariness, thought of home. Mimi's group would be rehearsing. They would be laughing and joking and warm, and at the right time Mama would come in with a tray of hot chocolate and cookies.

Becky had been walking slower and slower and as the girls strode ahead through a grove of birch trees, she thought she ought to catch up with them. Snow was falling earnestly now, the thick white flakes spinning down, and the limbs of the trees were building up layers of snow. Suddenly a sound made her stop in her tracks. Turning around, she found herself facing a roan horse who stood in the snow behind a barbed wire fence.

A real horse! That it was, not an illusion. Becky walked over to him and stood close while he regarded her with moist brown eyes.

"Hello, you beautiful, beautiful . . . ," Becky stopped, embarrassed. How do you talk to a horse, she wondered.

"You must be hungry," Becky said. She looked around and found a clump of grass half hidden by the snow. She picked what she could of it and held it out to him on the flat of her hand. His lips stretched over her offering and it disappeared in one greedy bite.

If only she had something else to give him. She was sorry she left the sandwich behind, but maybe he'd like an egg or an orange? She offered him her lunch, but he wasn't interested.

"Smart horse!" Becky said.

Timidly she reached up and touched him on the cheek. She passed her hand down his long nose and he seemed content with her attention.

"You *are* a lovely horse. I wish I could always be with you. I'd take such good care of you. I'd curry you and feed you and we would ride every day. How I would love you!"

She touched the soft black forelock that fell between his eyes and he nodded as if he understood what she was saying. Never had Becky been so content. She forgot that she had been weary and cold.

A whistle sounded from behind the grove of pines and birches. The horse pricked up his ears, then turned and disappeared through the woods while Becky watched. Then she turned around.

She was alone, all alone.

"Gosh! I forgot all about the girls. Where'd they go?"

She had strayed from the track to pet the horse and now she returned to where she thought it might be. But new snow covered the path. She walked where she thought the path might be, refusing to believe that she could be lost.

"But if I am lost," she reasoned, "Eileen or Gaby would find me." Comforting as the thought was, still it would be embarrassing to have to be found. So she hurried on ahead to try to catch up with Freckles.

The woods seemed endless, but at last she came to an open space and a narrow road. Should she go left or right or follow straight through the woods? The sky had become a vast white blanket and the snowflakes fell as if they would come down forever. The silence made a sound of its own, broken only by the occasional snapping of a twig or a bird crying in the distance. Once she thought she heard voices, but when she turned in the direction from which they seemed to come, there was only the sound of the distant wind.

Then perhaps she was the one who should call.

"Freckles! Hey, Freckles! Eileen! Gaby!"

How odd her voice sounded, quavery and lonesome in the quiet woods and somehow not like her voice at all. She was answered only by an echo, which made her feel lonelier than ever. She tried again and became frightened by the urgency in her voice.

"Freckles, where are you? It's me, Becky. I'm lost. Freckles!"

Her voice died in the wind and now she knew that she was really frightened. What if I'm the last person left on earth, she wondered. And what if they do forget me or do not care, and what if I never get out of this place? Why, I could die, I could really die.

They were dying in Europe like this, weren't they, those who were escaping? Only there would be soldiers shooting at them. And they would be even more lost, trying to find the borders of another country. She shivered and then began to shake and could not stop.

The cold passed through all the layers of her clothing, scarf and all, and seemed to penetrate to her very bones. Her teeth chattered and could not stop. Her feet were rapidly becoming icy stumps and now she realized she could actually *freeze* to death. Better keep walking, better keep moving.

She called again, but this time her voice broke and the snow muffled the unfinished cry. Not able to decide whether to go right or left, she thought that possibly the path continued through the woods on the other side of the road and it would be best to follow it. How endless the woods were! She had never known there was so much wild land in Connecticut. At last she saw an open spot and headed for it eagerly, as a wild hope that she would now find the girls lifted her fainting courage. But when she pushed the snapping branches aside and made her way to the open place, there were no girls, no signs, no tracks. While she stood there, she noticed three birches on one side and the stump of a tree close by. With a sinking feeling she realized this was where she had stood before. She had walked through the woods in a circle.

Now she was really lost. Never in all her life had she been so miserable. Or so scared. Tears began to sting her eyes and though she intended to blink them back, they rolled down her cheeks.

A noise broke the silence, a quiet sound of scurrying in

the brush, and Becky held her breath, then let it out gratefully as a rabbit jumped out of the woods. He was as surprised to see her as she was to see him; he looked at her questioningly and then disappeared up the road.

"I'll follow him," Becky thought and then she felt the warm spread of new hope.

The soft brown rabbit, already out of sight, had given her a direction. The road was bound to lead somewhere, and if it didn't take her to the girls, eventually it would offer a farmhouse where she might be allowed to rest, or to a paved road where a passing driver might give her a ride back to Hartford. She was beginning to feel better now, although the dirt road did seem to go on endlessly.

She thought she heard voices, but this time vowed she would not be fooled. Still, they did not stop. It was a garbled sound punctuated now and then by a high-pitched laugh.

No, she wasn't dreaming. She couldn't have imagined a sound like this. Taking new hope, she hurried toward the sound. The road made a sharp curve, and as she rounded it she saw the girls. She stopped, trying to catch her breath, and control the overwhelming sense of gratitude that welled up in her.

The girls were clustered around a fire near an open shed with a roof held up by four poles, which must be the "chalet." Freckles was hovering over the fire and when she looked up and saw Becky, she spoke calmly,

"Oh, it's you? Why didn't you keep up with us?"

But Eileen ran up and put her arm around Becky. "Don't mind Freckles. She's awful. She said you wanted to be alone. Is that true, or were you lost?"

"It wasn't anything really," Becky said, not wanting to cause a fuss.

"You must be starved. Let me help you with lunch,"

Gaby said. Then seeing Becky's experience had been a difficult one, she smiled in such a friendly way, that Becky even managed to smile back. "Now then, you make a tiny hole near the top of the orange and peel it around that hole, but not too much. Can you get the pulp out? Good, you eat that. Then you use the skin for a little pot: see, you break your egg in it and roast it in the fire."

Becky ate the orange pulp greedily and then broke the egg into the hollowed orange skin and placed it in the ashes. At the end of ten minutes the egg was still fairly raw and several ashes had fallen into it. Doxie called out that they would start back in three minutes. Becky tried to eat the egg but it was too raw and made her sick.

But she was content merely to sit on a stump of a tree and rest. And she no longer felt so cold or lost.

Just as her aching legs began to rest, Doxie blew a piercing blast on her whistle. It was time to hike back home.

"Becky! Oh my poor darling! Look at you!" Mama cried as Becky dragged herself up the stairs and fell into Papa's chair, unable to take one more step. It was already dark outside.

Mama fussed about Becky like a mother hen with one chick. She helped her into a hot bath and then warm pajamas. She tucked her into bed.

"And now I'll make you something to eat. How about eggs, soft boiled eggs?"

"Mama, how can you? I never want to see an egg again. Or an orange either."

"But Becky, I thought you loved them."

Mama brought her a tray with hot cocoa and buttered toast, and while she ate it, her sisters and Papa stood around. She told them about the hike.

"I know. I should never have let you go. Such foolishness!"

"You don't understand, Mama. It was hard but it was wonderful too. The woods, the snow, the horse, that nice Gaby . . . it made me glad to be alive."

"That's right," Papa said, "Just to be alive is a blessing."

"And I think Becky is falling asleep, so let's leave her for a while," Mama said.

Becky nodded as she dozed off, a slow smile on her face. Never in all her life had she been so tired or ached so much. And yet she was somehow satisfied.

She woke up a short time later in her dark room. Everyone must have been in the kitchen for the familiar sounds of the family drifted into the bedroom. Papa had said something funny and Dori's high-pitched giggle and Mimi's full-throated laugh were comforting. Becky heard the slight clatter of dishes as Mama put dinner on the table, and Dori telling all about the movie she had seen and Papa saying "Sh, don't wake Becky. Talk softer." These sounds were sounds suddenly precious, for that afternoon Becky had been in danger of losing them forever.

How good everyone is, she thought. How good it is to be safe at home! And how good it is to love and to be loved!

And then she fell asleep and didn't wake up until the morning sun stretched across her bed.

13

Becky, the Convalescent

All day Sunday Becky stayed in bed with a cold and fever. One minute she burned and the next she shivered with cold. But as the fevers lessened and the shivering grew less intense, she found that there were unexpected advantages in being only slightly ill.

Because she had almost never been sick, the family was shocked into more concern than was probably necessary. But Becky enjoyed it. Papa insisted on propping up the pillows for her and adjusting the shades so she would get just enough light. Mama brought her cup after cup of hot tea with lemon, her cure for everything. Mimi brought in trays covered with freshly ironed napkins on which were placed such delicacies as a cup of custard or dainty triangles of toast. Dori brought in her dolls and read to Becky from her first grade reader.

Even Lisa heard that Becky was sick. About four o'clock she came to visit, bringing with her a movie magazine. She had so much to tell Becky, about how she had gone to a party the night before at her cousin's house, far from Hope Street, and she had had such a wonderful time and some of the boys there thought she was, "Well, you know, sort of cute." And then she asked Becky how she had caught such a cold and when Becky told her, she shook her head in bewilderment.

"I can't understand you, Becky. Why would you want to walk so far? And you're not even sorry?"

Becky smiled and lay back against the pillows. There was no use explaining it to Lisa. "Tell me more about the party," she said.

On Monday Becky reached that pleasant stage of illness when she was no longer uncomfortable and yet she was not quite well enough to go back to school.

The house was very quiet after Papa left for work and her sisters went to school. Slipping on the bathrobe her mother had made for her last Chanukah, a red woolly robe cut like a coachman's coat with gold braid and frog fastenings, Becky stood in the doorway of the kitchen.

The kitchen looked familiar and yet different somehow. As usual, the sewing machine was open; the half-sewn pieces of a blue-flowered dress covered the kitchen table and another dress hung on the dressmaker form that stood in the corner like a lady without a head. That was all familiar. What was different was Mama not bending over the iron or sitting at the sewing machine, but standing at the window with a cup of coffee in her hand. She was looking out and seeing nothing. Becky recognized all the signs for she knew them well. But Mama daydreaming? Becky would not have believed it had she not seen it.

"Hello, Mama."

"Becky, you're up? Are you feeling better? You look better. Darling, you should wear slippers because the floor is cold. And let me make you some breakfast."

Mama cleared the dress from the table, and while Becky ate her oatmeal, Mrs. Golden picked up a dress that needed hemming and sat at the table with her.

"It's funny to be home in the morning with everyone gone," Becky said, and then she asked, "What were you thinking when I came in?"

"Nothing much, just thoughts."

"Mama, you were daydreaming. I know."

"So you think only young people are allowed to have daydreams? Older people can dream too." She bit off a piece of thread as though to end the conversation, but Becky kept on with it.

"When you were my age, Mama, did you ever want something very much, something that seemed impossible?"

When Mama smiled, dimples appeared in her round cheeks.

"It's a long time since I was your age, but when I was twelve, maybe a little older, I had two dreams. Such foolish dreams, my mother used to tell me, because they couldn't come true, she said."

"But they did? What were they?"

"You really want to know? All right, I'll tell you. One of the dreams was not really so impossible and the other was ridiculous. The funny part is that the ridiculous one came true.

"You know we were living in a small village outside of Kiev. My father was a tailor and he taught me to sew when I was a little girl, like Dori. I had the gift for sewing. Well, one day . . . ."

The telephone rang and Becky had to wait while Mama made an appointment with Mrs. Reuben for a fitting. The story would take forever to be told, but Mama settled down again, took up her sewing, and continued.

"Where was I? One of my dreams, as you know, the crazy dream, was to come to America. Such things as we heard about it! But it was so expensive to get here and so difficult to get away, that where we were concerned it was an impossible wish. My other dream seemed more practical. One of my father's customers, a rich lady, took me to the ballet in Moscow one day and it was the most wonderful unbelievable spectacle I had ever seen. Like a magic fairy tale, Becky, so beautiful with dancers and music, the brilliant colors and the costumes. I fell in love with it."

Becky knew exactly what she meant. Mama's eyes shone even as she thought about it. She must have loved the ballet the way I love horses, Becky thought.

"Go on, Mama, what happened?"

"I kept dreaming of it and I decided that when I grew a little older, I would go to Moscow and become a part of the ballet. I couldn't dance, of course, but I could sew, and if they would let me work on the costumes, I knew I would be content. Only . . .

"You know, Becky. In our village there were rumblings and grumblings and one day the soldiers came and attacked us. They threw rocks through the windows and set the houses on fire; it was awful. That's when my mother was killed. You know, it was her locket you are wearing. Well, to make a long story short, we managed to escape and eventually I found my way to America. And here I am, only instead of sewing ballet costumes I'm making dresses for ladies, some of them very fat ladies and some of them very old and very dull."

She whispered this last so that Becky would know it was confidential. Mama held up the dress she was working on, a dull gray dress, beautifully cut and finished, but not the stylish colorful dress Mama would have preferred her customers to wear. Mama thought that all clothes should be handsome; that even a house dress could have a certain style. She believed old ladies should not wear only grays and blacks, but it was not easy to convince her customers.

"Poor Mama," Becky said.

"Poor Mama? Not at all," she said. "I have a good husband and three lovely daughters, good girls. And we are lucky to be living here in this country. You know what I mean, don't you? So I'm content."

"Yes, but Mama, then what were you dreaming about at the window just now?"

"Oh that? Something silly. Everyone has to have silly dreams but I don't know why."

"Like Papa wishing he had a boy?"

"You know about that, Becky? We never told you. We didn't want you to be hurt, you or your sisters."

Becky laughed. "It's no secret, Mama. We all know. And it's sure silly. You can't order baby boys."

"If I could have another baby, I would, just because your father would love to have a son. But the doctor says no more babies for me. Your father is more than happy with his three daughters. And the dream I have is the same way, nonsense maybe, but still I like to think of it."

Mama had never talked so much and Becky was fascinated. She seemed to want to confide in Becky.

"Tell me, Mama," Becky urged her.

"First you must realize, I am grateful for everything we have, for the roof over our head, the bread on the table. So I'm not complaining."

Becky nodded. "But . . . ," she began her mother's next sentence.

"But," Mrs. Golden smiled at her, "if we could have a little house of our own, maybe not out in the country but toward the edge of the city so we could have a small garden with vegetables and flowers, and maybe you and Mimi and Dori could each have a little room of your own, and where we don't hear the neighbors fight so much and where the streets are clean and there are trees. Just a little house, white with blue shutters, and we'd have roses in front."

"That's not so impossible, is it, Mama? Could I keep a horse?"

"Who knows?" Mrs. Golden said, squinting a little as she

threaded the needle. "If I get the house, I guess you can have the horse. Can you keep a secret? Sure, you can. I know that. All right, Becky, sometimes I make a few dollars sewing and I put it away. It's called a nest egg and I think someday it will hatch, and we'll have our house. But something always happens and I have to use the money. Last year Grandpa needed an operation and that took everything. And when Papa is out of work, there's no choice; sometimes we have to use it to pay the rent and to have something to eat. But we always begin again. Maybe someday there'll be enough."

"Someday, Mama, I'll bet there will be. I just know there will."

Mama smiled at her daughter. "What an optimist you are! That's good. Otherwise there just isn't any hope."

With that, Mrs. Golden finished the last bit of the hem and turned to her sewing machine. Becky, stirring her chocolate, thought about wishes and how odd they were. Sometimes the impossible ones worked out, but they were not really just what had been expected, such as Mimi's hair having unexpected results and Mama's coming to America being a blessing. And yet Mama's life in America wasn't all that she had dreamed.

The doorbell rang. "Oh my, I almost forgot. I have a new customer today, a Mrs. Schultz," Mama said, jumping up.

She hurried to go down the front stairs and let her in, and Becky rushed into her bedroom, shutting the door behind her.

14

Becky's Mural

Sitting cross-legged on her bed, Becky considered her room. For the first time in her life she saw it objectively as a stranger might see it. Before this she had always taken it for granted as the room where she slept, kept her clothes and her prizes. But perhaps because of Mama's wish for her girls to have separate bedrooms or because Becky had been in the room all the day before, she looked at her room more critically and was not pleased.

She wondered why she had never noticed before that the linoleum on the floor was poorly patched and discolored, and the cracks in the wall now seemed to glare at her in jagged ugliness. Becky's and Mimi's beds were different sizes and the headboards were quite dissimilar although Mama had tried to unify them by making identical bedspreads.

"Mimi's half of the room looks better than mine," Becky pondered. Although the wallpaper on her side was faded as Becky's and the linoleum was as crudely patched, still there were touches that only Mimi would have made. Her dressing table with its filmy skirt, the "bedside table" (another orange crate but this time covered with wallpaper) topped with a collection of perfume bottles and glass animals from the five and ten, and a series of colored ribbons hanging on the wall seemed to announce that this was Mimi's part of the room. Over her bed were photographs of three actresses, all of them brunette, replacing the blondes who had been there until the unfortunate day when Mimi decided to become a blonde.

"And my side of the room is nothing, just nothing," Becky said. And yet, what could she do about it? Dressing tables, photographs of glamorous movie stars, and perfume bottles were not for her. But she could have pictures on the wall.

She pulled out a box from under her bed and opened it. Her collection of horses—the work of more than three years—was stored in this box. Hundreds, perhaps a thousand, pictures of horses had been snipped from magazines, newspapers, the old movie magazines from Mrs. Kirby's beauty parlor, and even illustrations from a badly battered old copy of *Black Beauty*. Some of the collection measured tinier than Becky's smallest fingernail and the largest covered an entire page of a newspaper.

Three pictures over her bed would match the three actresses over Mimi's bed. That would be a start. After grave consideration, for it wasn't easy to make choices, she decided on a glossy photograph she had won in a contest of a famous race horse. The second selection was a white circus horse with its bespangled rider, part of a poster advertising a circus. The third choice, a palomino, was difficult, for although this was her favorite horse, he had a gash in his side where she had cut out the package of cigarettes in the advertisement.

Checking to see that Mama and the new customer were still in the bedroom for a fitting, Becky tiptoed to the kitchen. Quickly she made paste out of flour and water and dashed back to her room and shut the door.

In less than two minutes the three horses were pasted over her bed and she stepped back to look at them.

"Not bad!" she praised herself. "If only I had a frame for them."

This first success led to further inspiration. A border of tiny pictures all the same size put around the larger photos would have the same effect as a frame. This project took a longer time than the first, as she trimmed the smaller pictures to postage stamp size and pasted them up, using Mama's yardstick to keep them straight. At last the frame was complete and she stepped back to see what she had done. She clasped her hands and almost squealed. It was perfect! It worked! It looked like a frame.

Now what? Well, she reasoned, if a few horses look that good, wouldn't more be even better? Better than the faded scarred wallpaper surely.

Once Mama knocked on the door. "Lunchtime, Becky!"

"Don't come in," she cried. "I'll be out in a second."

By three o'clock, two walls were completely covered with horses. Generously, she pasted the best ones over Mimi's bed. Next to the actress with the sultry expression as she looked over a bare shoulder, Becky placed an anatomical study of a horse showing his bones and muscles. The rear view of a percheron flanked the other actress. And a row of drawings showing the developing stages of horse's teeth fit neatly across the top.

Becky was delighted. "It's terrific," she exclaimed. "A complete collection!" Society ladies in jodhpurs and bowlers on aristocratic show horses mingled with poor wretched nags pulling wagons. A colt looked out shyly as he stood by his mother in a pasture and horses on parade with colored plumes on their heads marched across the wall over the bureau. The proud white Lippizaner stallions, a sculpture of a Chinese horse, a team of Clydesdales pulling a brewery wagon, a soft-eyed Shetland pony, a horse shying at a car, Princess Elizabeth sitting proudly side-saddle, and endless western movie stars posing with their famous steeds.

Satisfied and exhausted, for she really had been sick, Becky fell back on her bed. The walls looked fresh and new, all the cracks and discolored wallpaper hidden.

"I'll just take a little nap," she promised, "and then I'll do the other two walls." She shut her eyes and immediately fell into a deep and contented sleep.

An hour later a screaming elder sister jerked her into wakefulness.

"Mama, Mama, come here. Look what Becky's done to our room. Just look, Ma. It's terrible. Oh you, Becky, you. When I think of the custard I made for you yesterday and the way I brought you the trays, and now . . . and now . . . ," she sputtered with anger at Becky who sat up in bed, her mouth open with innocence. It wasn't possible. Mimi didn't seem to like what she had done.

Mama rushed to the room not knowing what to expect. Her first reaction was a sigh of relief.

"All that screaming for this? How you scared me, Mimi. I thought the room was on fire or . . . well, something much worse. Thank God you're both all right."

"Mama, look at those pictures. I will not have horses in my room. I will not. Not in my half. Look at those nasty things over my bed."

Her eyes flashed with anger as she reached up and tore the rear view of the percheron in half while Becky wailed.

"Not that one, not that one! It's one of the best. Look what you've done, you idiot! I worked all day on this. I gave you my best, my *very best,* pictures."

"Mama, make her take those things off the wall. I won't have them."

"Girls, stop fighting. Be calm. We can settle this."

Becky's jaw stuck out and a hard light came into her eyes. Even if Mimi had made her hot chocolate and custard the day before, she wasn't going to be bought off. And besides, it was her room as well as Mimi's. Her voice fell to a dangerous determined level.

"No. I'm not taking down a single picture."

"Mama, she put a horse's behind right next to Katharine Hepburn. And all those horse's teeth. Ugh!"

Mama looked at her girls, the one angry and the other stubborn, and now her voice became stern.

"Enough is enough! I don't want to hear another word. Becky is sick. Mimi is angry. And it's four o'clock and I think if we all sit down and have a cup of hot tea, we'll discuss the pictures afterward."

"You're going to take down every one of those pictures," Mimi threatened in a stage whisper, as though Mama couldn't hear.

"I am *not!*" Becky whispered back just as fiercely.

Before the battle reached another crescendo, a tiny voice called out, "Mama, where are you, Mama? Guess what!" Dori danced in, too excited to notice her sisters or the new decorations on the wall.

"I got a new friend and she lives in Margie's old house. Come in, Mickey. Come in, honey. Don't be afraid."

Dori had to coax her new friend again, and at last a leprechaun of a child drifted in. Mama, Mimi, and Becky said hello politely and stopped in confusion. Who . . . or what . . . was this child Dori had brought home.

It was a very tiny child with a delicate quality, and yet it seemed to swagger. It was impossible to tell if it was a boy or a girl. A black beret pulled down over its forehead stopped directly above two bright darting eyes and the coat that the child wore was held together with a large safety pin. The blue eyes that moved from Mimi to Becky to Mama and finally rested on Dori were alert as a sparrow's.

Mama knew just what to do. "It's four o'clock and we could all do with a cup of tea. And today I made cookies, so let's go in the kitchen, everybody. All right?"

It was a peculiar teatime, with the older girls still angry about the room yet fascinated by the tiny gnome that Dori seemed to have adopted. When Mickey remarked that Mimi's hair was "priddy with all dose stripes," Mimi was taken aback, but Mickey repeated that Mimi was "orfully priddy" and Mimi softened.

Mama knew more about Mickey than her daughters did. This was truly a Depression child, one who had never known what it was to have enough to eat or decent clothes to wear or the security of a home. As Mama watched Mickey stuff one cookie into her mouth after another, she was already thinking that some of Dori's outworn clothes would fit her and that after tea she would sew a button on her coat.

Becky was realizing something very different. "So Dori's wish has come true. She wanted a friend to replace Margie, and this one even lives in the same house. Mimi's wish happened, and now Dori's; maybe I'll be next."

The wonder of it made the back of her neck prickle with anticipation and later, when she and Mimi were discussing what to do about the room, she found it did not matter to her very much and even offered to take down the horses from Mimi's side of the room. She even hummed to herself as she peeled off the photographs carefully, so as not to rip them, because what was going to happen was so much more important than decorating a room. Mimi was puzzled.

"What are you so happy about?" she asked.

But Becky only smiled mysteriously. "You'll find out when it's the right time!" she said and refused to explain what she meant.

15

A Letter

Becky had what her father called mailbox fever. Even though she knew the winners of the Wonder contest would not be announced until the end of April, still she looked through the mail as soon as she came home from school and frequently carried it upstairs when Mama had been too busy to pick it up.

When there was nothing but the thin familiar letter from Austria with its delicate European script, she was almost tempted to keep it from her father. At one time Cousin Bernard's letters made Papa so happy he would read them out loud at the dinner table, translating as he went.

"Anna is teaching David music and I think he will be a good musician. Little as he is, he can already play some of the easier Mozart pieces, but it's too early to boast. I also hope he will be a good fisherman."

or

"In spite of all the political troubles in Germany and all the fears here, our concerts are going well. Tomorrow there will be a special program in a hall inside one of the lovely palaces here. I wish your girls could see it. Afterward there will be a reception."

or

"Anna, David, and I went for a picnic today in the Prater, which, as you know, is one of the lovely Vienna parks. How

we wish all of you could have been with us! Perhaps someday we will all be together."

More than once Bernard had enclosed snapshots and Becky could see that his wife Anna was very sweet as she sat holding a tiny boy with large velvety eyes, and Bernard himself looked very professional in a formal photograph where he held his violin.

But now the letters made Papa even more silent and grim than when he listened to the news over the radio each night or when he read the newspapers after dinner. Papa had something else to worry about as well, for the place where he worked threatened to close down and then he would be out of work again. To worry about that and also Cousin Bernard was asking too much of him.

But the letter belonged to Papa and there was no question about his getting it. Reluctantly, Becky placed it next to the sugar bowl on the kitchen table where he would see it when he came in that evening.

Papa read the letter, folded it and put it in his pocket.

"What does it say?" Mama asked.

"Nothing very much," Papa said, but he looked more worried than usual. It was no secret that the Jews in Vienna were treated even worse than those in Germany. They were made to wash the streets and submit to all kinds of indignities; their businesses were taken from them; they were rounded up to be sent away; many had committed suicide. Such stories were not in the newspapers, but those fortunate souls who could emigrate from Europe had told of the horrors they had seen, and feared that things would get worse.

After dinner, Papa sat in his favorite chair and Becky, seeing how withdrawn he looked, perched on the arm of his chair and put her arm around him. He tried to be cheerful.

"Well, Becky, it seems to me there's a holiday coming up. What do you think?"

"Sure, Papa. Passover. Next week."

"Of course, and a sober one it will be, I'm afraid. But I'm thinking of another very special day. What do you suppose?"

Poor Papa, Becky was thinking. He was trying so hard to be a good father and not burden his daughters with all his fears.

"I know," Dori cried. "It's Becky's birthday. You knew it all along, Papa."

"So it is," Papa said. "And she's going to be twelve, right?"

"Thirteen, Papa. You know it, don't pretend," Dori cried.

"Well now, that's pretty special. What shall we get you for a present, Becky?"

Mama coughed loudly but it was too late. She had warned Papa not to ask Becky, because Becky would ask for a horse. Becky looked down, not knowing what to say. There was only one thing she wanted.

"You know, Papa."

"No, I don't know. I can't even guess. Remember when Dori asked for 20,000 ice cream cones?"

"Sure, and remember what Dori got," Mama said.

"Just what she asked for," Papa said. "She got the first five and gave one to everyone in the family. Only 19,995 to go."

"Papa, you're laughing at me. I was only a little girl then."

"And remember when I asked for a fur coat?" Mimi had been six years old then, the very worst of the Depression, and Papa could hardly pay the rent.

"And so Mama found a scrap of fur and sewed it to the collar of my coat," Mimi went on proudly. "And I got what

I wanted." She never let on that she had cried secretly because she had wanted an entire coat of white bunny fur.

"And what do you want, Becky? Anything your heart desires!" he said. He was trying so hard to be cheerful. If Becky told him, he would laugh at her, she knew, but maybe it would get his mind off the letter.

"Becky wants a HORSE. Don't you know that?" Dori cried.

"I guess if you gave Dori her ice cream cones in installments, you can give me the horse that way too. A tail this week, a mane next week . . . ." Becky could joke too, but under the joking was her anxiety.

"Where do you get these ideas, Becky? From my people, my family? Never. Must be your mother's family is so rich they have stables, full of horses. Uncle Jonas, for example . . . ."

"Now you leave him out of this," Mama cried. More than once she had to dig into her nest egg to help Jonas out of an unfortunate matter of lost bets at the racetrack, but she would have no criticism of him.

Mimi came to Becky's defense.

"You shouldn't make fun of her, Papa. Lots of girls like horses. They're beautiful animals. She really ought to have one."

Papa raised his eyebrows in surprise.

"What a strange disease," he said. "When I was a boy, girls liked boys. Now they like horses. What is the world coming to?"

The letter rattled in his pocket as he shifted his weight. The conversation became strained; it had gone far enough.

"Papa," Becky said, "tell me, what did Cousin Bernard write?"

The smile Papa had been attempting vanished and he took out the letter and held it, though he knew it by heart.

"Do you really want to know?" he asked.

Becky wanted most of all not to know, but she said, "Yes."

"Bernard writes that the world has indeed changed and that it is difficult to write very much about it. He still plays in the orchestra but all the other members of the string quartet he played in—well, he doesn't know where they are or what has happened to them. He writes that he loves us all and that his dearest wish is that we will all be together again. That's all, Becky. It's a short letter. It's what he doesn't say or cannot say, that I worry about."

"You think the secret police would read his mail?"

"It's possible. There is almost nothing I cannot believe any more." Papa folded the letter carefully and put it back in his pocket, as though it were a precious document. Becky reached for any wisp of hope that would encourage her father, for she could hardly bear to see him looking so unhappy.

"But Papa, maybe he will be a very special case and they won't torture him because he's such a great violinist. They might be afraid of what other countries would think, or maybe they just want to hear him play."

Papa patted her hand and shook his head. "Anything is possible, Becky, anything. Maybe you're right. Just maybe." But the despair in his eyes suggested that he found it hard to believe.

That night Becky dreamed. It was her birthday and everyone was sitting in the living room, waiting for something to happen.

"It will be here at seven. I can hardly wait," Mimi said.

"But the clock has stopped. Look!" Becky cried in chagrin, as though it were vastly important.

Papa walked over to the clock, touched it with one finger

and it began to run again. "You know you can't stop time," he said.

It took forever for the minute hand to turn to seven, but once the bells began to announce the time, there was a stamping at the door and Becky flung it open. There stood her horse, the palomino. A wind blew his sunbleached mane gently. There was never any question of where he had come from or how he had climbed the stairs. Nor was there any question that he was meant for her.

She mounted the horse without any difficulty whatever, as though she had done this every day of her life. She waved good-by to everyone and then the horse floated through the open air to the moonlit plain below. She rode easily, cloppeta-cloppeta through the chilly night. Never had she been so at peace as she moved far away from home and from Hope Street.

Once she turned to wave good-by to her family who stood in the doorway. Mama was wiping her eyes with a tiny handkerchief and Mimi and Dori were waving and crying good-by, but their voices were lost in the wind. She thought she saw flames rising behind them, but still she rode faster and faster toward the far horizon while her family grew smaller and smaller and were finally lost to sight.

When Becky woke up in the morning she was puzzled about the dream, and alarmed. Where was she going? And what were the flames she saw? Was it a good dream, or a bad dream? Certainly it was mixed. As the morning passed, she found herself remembering her ride on the palomino and how easily they had floated through the open air. It was a good sign, she concluded. Her horse would surely come.

16

A Birthday

Becky was glad when Passover was over. Usually it was a thoughtful but happy celebration when all the aunts and uncles and cousins met at the Goldens. Leaves were put in the table to accommodate everyone who came. But this year, it was a long solemn time and when the ancient wish was repeated, Next year in Jerusalem!, a sober silence fell in the room.

But the Passover holidays had passed, and now something else was going on, but Becky was left out of it. More than once she found Mimi and her mother whispering together, only to talk loudly and unconvincingly about something else as soon as they saw Becky. Dori and Mickey, who almost seemed like a fourth daughter in the house, burst into fits of giggles every time they saw Becky.

"What's so funny?" she asked over and over, but they only clapped their hands over their mouths and giggled all the more.

With only a week before her birthday, Becky was suspicious. For a wild moment she wondered if Papa had found a horse for her and made arrangements with a stable to keep it? After all, he had been working for a while. And then again, he might have found a bargain in the way of a horse. One never knew what would happen where Papa was concerned.

At last her birthday came, a sunny morning, the first Saturday in May. The breakfast table had been carefully set with a pink tablecloth. Dori had picked a bouquet of daisies from an empty lot and put them in a glass of water and Mama had prepared Becky's favorite breakfast, fresh strawberries with thick sour cream and sugar on top. Becky was genuinely pleased.

"Thank you everybody, thank you. This is really nice."

The day seemed to belong to her even though she helped with the breakfast dishes and made the beds as she did on other Saturday mornings.

"What's the matter with all of you? What's the big *joke?*" she finally asked. Everyone seemed to be grinning so idiotically.

Mama changed the subject. "Since it's your birthday, do you want to go to the movies this afternoon, Becky? It's a good show. Dori will go with you."

Why did Mama make such a point of it, just as though she didn't take Dori to the movies most Saturdays.

"I don't know, Mama. I don't think I'll go. It's so nice outside and today is my birthday. So I want it to be different, not like other Saturdays."

"Oh," Mama's face seemed to fall. "But I thought you loved movies."

"I do, Mama, I do. I just don't want to waste my birthday."

"Sure, whatever you say, Becky. It *is* your day," Mama's voice seemed to weaken and Becky saw her exchange an intense glance with Mimi. She was getting tired of all the mystery.

Later that morning Mama asked Becky for a favor. "I know it's your birthday, *liebchen*, but your Great-aunt Martha isn't feeling well. She's such an old lady. Do you think maybe you could take something to her from me?

Barley soup and stuffed cabbage. It's her favorite food and it's all made."

"Mama, on my birthday? Heck, she lives on the other side of the city."

"That's right. If you don't want to go, never mind. Nobody's making you go. But I thought you would like to go. You're her favorite, but don't tell the others that. And of course I would give you bus fare."

Becky slouched in a chair, her feet stretched out in front. After deliberating for five minutes, she said, "All right. I suppose so."

"That's a good girl and that's a good deed you'll be doing. And if you want to wear your red dress, that would be nice too."

Now Mama was going too far.

"Mama, it's enough that I'm going. What's wrong with pants?"

"Those pants that belonged to a boy, your Cousin Louis? Well, it's your day and if you want to wear them, all right. I won't argue."

The bag of groceries was heavy enough. Two jars of soup, the cabbage rolls, a small loaf of bread, and some strudel.

"She sure has a fine appetite for a sick old lady," Becky said.

But Becky's disappointment vanished once she was outdoors. The day itself was like a birthday present. She walked several city blocks and then cut through the park to get to the bus stop. Everything seemed to promise a blooming, the fuzzy green leaves new on the tree and tiny white daisies sparkling in the grass. The whole world seemed to be celebrating her birthday.

Aunt Martha—really Great-aunt Martha, for she was her father's aunt—was spry enough for an old lady who was supposed to be ailing. She kissed Becky on both cheeks, stood back, and said what a fine girl she was and how pretty.

"Tell me, do you have a boyfriend, Becky?"

"No," Becky replied with scorn. As if she even wanted one!

Becky gave Aunt Martha Mama's package and started to leave, but Aunt Martha said she had something for her. But first she unpacked the bag of food, and had to admire and comment on every single thing. How slow old people are, Becky thought, as if they have all the time in the world.

Then Aunt Martha disappeared into the bedroom and when she came out, walking very slowly and uncertainly because she really was very old, she held an ancient photograph album in her hand. Becky let a sigh escape before she could stop it. Was she going to have to spend her whole birthday looking through that thing?

But there was no getting out of it without hurting Aunt Martha's feelings, so they sat on the sofa together and looked at family pictures. Mama and Papa on their wedding day; an austere family portrait in Russia, with the women's hair puffed out on their heads and the men wearing fur hats; a photograph of her father as a somber baby in an embroidered white dress. The pictures lacked order, yet Becky caught a glimpse of a different world in another time at another place. How odd it was to think that she was related to all these people! There was even a photograph of Mama as a young girl, taken before her marriage. It was unbelievable that Mama could have once been a girl, only six years older than Becky was that very day.

"Who's this?" Becky asked as she picked up a photograph in brown sepia tones that were beginning to fade. The two boys in the picture might have been about fourteen years old, two boys with thick coal-black hair and large sensitive eyes.

"You don't know who those boys are?" Aunt Martha asked, and when Becky shook her head, Aunt Martha explained. "It's your father and his cousin, Bernard. You never saw such friends in all your life. They were closer than brothers, and full of mischief, but serious too. Bernard was a fine musician, probably a genius. And your father learned watchmaking from his father when he was still a boy. And when your father and Bernard got together. . . ." A smile bloomed on Aunt Martha's face and she shook her head slightly as though recalling something long past.

"Becky, would you like to have this picture? I want you to choose any one you would like as my gift to you."

"Could I, Aunt Martha? I would love it. I never knew my father was so good looking. Bernard looks just like him."

"Sure, it's a family look. The Golden look. Wait, Becky, I have an antique frame I want to give you. I think the photograph will fit inside."

Now when Aunt Martha walked slowly into the bedroom, Becky could see that it was painful for her to walk and she was ashamed for having been so impatient. Aunt Martha returned with a frame and fit the photograph in it with trembling fingers and then carefully wrapped it in brown paper.

"How about some candy, Becky? Would you like soda or some cookies?"

Becky refused politely, wanting to leave, yet staying while the old lady filled a bag with hard paper-wrapped candies for her. Becky kissed her good-by, held the parcel under her arm, and finally left. She looked up from the sidewalk and saw Aunt Martha standing at the window. She waved and this time she felt very warm toward Great-aunt Martha.

17

Surprise!

Becky ran up the front stairs, hoping Papa would be home so she could show him the photograph. She opened the door and before she could call out a loud chorus startled her:

SURPRISE! SURPRISE! SURPRISE!

Girls seemed to pop up from all over the living room, from behind chairs and the lumpy brown sofa, all of her friends grinning and shouting in high giddy voices. The somber parlor with one rubber plant as its chief ornament had been transformed to an unbelievable display of color. Twisted strips of pink and orange crepe paper were festooned from one end of the room to the other, balloons of every shape and color hung from the ceiling, and a pouf of thinly cut strips of paper blossomed out of the chandelier.

HAPPY BIRTHDAY, BECKY! HAPPY BIRTHDAY!

Becky's mouth dropped. A surprise party! She'd heard of them but had never attended one, and here was everyone having it for her. Mimi, Dori, two of her cousins and three more who had driven in from Middletown, Lisa Kline, and Eileen Dolan stood around Becky applauding and grinning, each of them dressed in their party best. Even Mickey was there, scrubbed and shining and looking very much like a proper little girl in an outgrown party dress of Dori's.

Mama, who was standing in the doorway, was as excited as Becky. She had never known what a birthday party was in her own childhood, and it would not have occurred to Mama to give a party if Mimi hadn't persuaded her because it was Becky's thirteenth birthday. "A boy would have a Bar Mitzvah and a big party," Mimi said. "So can't we have just a birthday party for Becky?" So with Mimi's ideas and Aunt Clara's help, Mama was more than delighted to arrange a surprise party for Becky.

The room was shaking with noise as everyone talked at once. A dance record on the old windup phonograph added to the din.

"Hey, Becky, I got a present for ya. Open it quick, huh, willya!" Mickey had to shout to be heard as she tugged at Becky's pants. She held up a brown paper bag and Becky could see a wet spot spreading on it. Aunt Clara bent over and spoke to Mickey.

"The presents go on the coffee table, Mickey, with all the other presents. And Becky will open them after we play games."

"B-bbbbut . . .," Mickey looked worried and Mimi stepped in.

"Aunt Clara, I think this present ought to be opened right away fast."

Becky looked into the bag while Mickey jumped up and down in her excitement. Then Becky pulled out a kitten, a tiny waif of a creature with soft gray fur and round blue eyes. It rested on Becky's outstretched palm, looked around, and let out a mystified Meow!

"How sweet!"

"What a darling!"

Everyone cooed over the thin little cat.

"Mama, can I keep him, please, Mama?"

Becky, Mimi, and Dori all looked at Mama with pleading

eyes, for Mama had always been strict about not allowing animals in the house. Becky put the kitten in her hands, and Mama confessed she had never held a kitten in her hand before.

"It's only a baby," she said, and apparently she was touched by the trusting innocence of the little creature for she added, "Of course you can keep her. Such a nice present for Mickey to give you! But I think she's scared with so many people watching her. Let me give her some milk in the kitchen, the darling. Listen, she's purring!"

Mickey was so happy she could hardly get the words out. "He hungry. I foun' him in the street. All alone. No mama. He like me. He like you too."

Becky bent down to give Mickey a kiss.

"You are really sweet. And guess what, I'm going to name the cat Mickey, just like you!"

Mickey beamed and Becky caught her radiating excitement. "Right now I'm perfectly happy," she thought, and then amended it to "almost."

From that moment on everything happened so fast it was like an early silent movie where the action is jerky, speeded up beyond recognition and not quite real. Becky still could not believe that this was a party just for her. In a daze she played games with the other girls and afterward sat at the place of honor in the dining room while Mama brought out a huge birthday cake, decorated with pink icing and a circle of frosting roses. Becky thought that she was a little old for the candy baskets and colored paper hats that Mama had bought, but realized that Mama didn't know they would be more suitable for someone of Dori's age. And then again maybe thirteen wasn't too old after all. Everyone was having a great time and even Becky enjoyed blowing the long party whistle Aunt Clara had brought.

Mimi, who seemed to know exactly how such matters were handled, told Becky that she must kneel on the floor and open the gifts one by one. Her face russet with the amazement of the whole afternoon, Becky became the center of attention as she slowly and carefully opened each pretty package. A chorus of "oh's" and "ah's" greeted the book of horse stories, the scarlet chiffon scarf, the pin shaped like a riding crop, and the pink bra and panty set from Aunt Clara which made Becky turn an even deeper pink. At that point Papa, who had been standing in the background looking on, placed a long thin box on the table. Becky had seen boxes that shape for so long, she knew what it would be, and hugged her father before she opened it. And then she gasped, for she had not dreamed what a handsome watch it would be.

"Oh Papa, it's the most, it's the loveliest. . . ."

"It won't quack like your Donald Duck watch," Papa said, "I tried and tried, but I just couldn't manage that quack."

"He's only joking," Mama explained to the company although the Goldens knew that Papa could not endure Becky's loud Donald Duck watch she had won in a contest long ago. Papa's eyes were bright with satisfaction as he saw that Becky was more than pleased with the watch. "He worked on that watch a whole year, Becky, all those little wheels and discs and heaven knows what . . . a whole year to make that watch just for you."

"It was only an hour here, an hour there," Papa said modestly.

"Oh Papa—I love it!" She hugged him again.

Where the time went, nobody knew, but soon the girls were saying good-by and thank you for such a nice time.

"It was a wonderful party and they did have a good time," Aunt Clara said. "They didn't want to leave."

Becky collapsed in a chair. Content, perfectly content, and still not able to believe what had happened. Mickey purred in her lap. She almost fell asleep, but the doorbell rang insistently and then someone knocked vigorously on the door. Becky, dazed, heard the clock strike, looked at her new watch, and saw it was exactly seven o'clock.

Seven o'clock on her birthday! The dream rushed back at her. Now she knew that all day long a voice had whispered to her over and over again, "Wait, Becky, it's coming! Wait, Becky, today is the day! You'll see, Becky!" It hadn't been Aunt Martha's gift, or the surprise party, or even Papa's watch, lovely as it was, but "something more," the voice promised.

The rapping on the door was repeated. But it can't be a horse, Becky argued with herself. In a dream anything was believable, but she wasn't dreaming now. And yet, and yet, and yet . . . she argued with herself, what else could it be but a horse. Perhaps a man telling her that her horse was waiting for her in the street down below.

Now the rapping grew louder, more insistent. "Becky, would you please see who it is?" her mother called.

"Okay, I'll get it," she yelled as she ran to the door.

No horse. Only Uncle Jonas standing there grinning, a western hat in one hand and a bouquet of roses in the other. He put them in Becky's arms while she stood there blinking.

"Happy birthday and a greeting for the birthday girl!" he said gallantly. "Well, aren't you going to ask me in, Becky?"

She recovered. No horse. Only Uncle Jonas and those roses. "Are they for me? They're so pretty. Nobody ever gave me roses before so I'm a little surprised."

She began to laugh. At first it was pleasant, but then she couldn't stop. How silly she had been to expect a horse, yet underneath all her common sense, she thought just possibly some kind of sign would show that indeed there was a horse for her somewhere, that very day. Caught in a fit of laughing and crying, Becky fell back on the sofa, holding her sides while everyone wondered what the joke was. Mama and Papa, however, were concerned. Becky hysterical? She recovered before they had to worry any more.

"Quite a day for you, isn't it, Becky?" Papa asked.

She nodded. Everything was so mixed up. The party, the kitten, the new watch, all her friends there, the streamers making the living room so joyful. And yet, why had she thought about the horse! A wish could be a burden.

The doorbell rang again and this time it was Uncle Charlie and Joey. Then others came, aunts, uncles, cousins, good friends. A formal invitation had not been necessary. Word got around that it was a special day, so everyone came bearing salads, platters of meats, freshly baked pastries, and bowls of fruit. The house was filled with laughing and talking and the sound of music.

And three hours later it still went on. Mimi and her young cousins were dancing in the living room to music from the radio. Dori, still white and fluffy in her party dress, fell asleep on the sofa in the middle of the din, and Becky wandered from one room to another, for the party seemed everywhere, and she was still dazed with everything that had happened that day. It was a noisy happy party with bursts of sudden laughter, and if the tragedy of Europe was purposely not mentioned, it was hardly forgotten, and from time to time someone would become unexpectedly sober. But this was Becky's night, and so the party must remain happy.

The night wore on and Becky sat beside Papa at the kitchen table where her aunts and uncles sat, drinking endless cups of tea and telling stories. Becky was tempted to show her father the photograph Aunt Martha had given her, but hesitated, for it would make him sad and at the moment he was chuckling at one of Uncle Jonas' inimitable amusing tales. Becky had not seen her father so relaxed for a long time, and she leaned her head against his shoulder, and yawned, for she was very sleepy, very content, very content indeed.

The horse had not come, but what did that matter? He would come another time, of that she was sure. For the moment she was very happy, and as the people around her talked, she fell asleep.

18

Pulling in the Belt

As Becky turned the corner of Hope Street on her way home from school the week after her birthday, she was surprised to see Mimi waiting for her. Becky was just as glad Lisa wasn't with her that day, for Mimi's face looked sober. A thousand possible tragedies coursed through Becky's head. Had something happened to Mama or Papa? Had the house caught on fire? Was Dori all right?

"Hi, Mimi, what's the matter?"

"Hi, Becky," Mimi talked with agonizing slowness. "Mama wanted me to talk to you before you got home."

"Well, tell me what it's all about. Don't take so long."

"Time to pull in the belt again. Papa's out of work. The store folded up."

"Oh that," Becky sighed in relief. Being out of work was not exactly good news, but it was nothing like the catastrophes she had just imagined. "Poor Papa! He was afraid of that. It's always so hard on him. But then he always finds something else."

"That's what Mama tells him, and a lot of good that does. Anyway, you know how crabby he gets when he's laid off, so Mama wanted me to warn you."

"Sure, thanks," Becky said. Mama had a whole code of behavior for those times when Papa was out of work. Becky imitated Mama as she walked along with Mimi. "Don't ask

Papa questions. Be cheerful, but not *too* cheerful. And if you act sad, that will make him feel worse. Don't complain. Don't suddenly feel you have to have a new pair of shoes or a box of caramels. And don't ask Papa when he's going back to work. Just be natural."

"That's the one that gets me," Mimi said. "Just be natural! When we're complaining or when we want something we can't have, that's the time we're most natural."

They walked slowly, both of them knowing just what to expect. Mama was usually cheerful, but now her cheerfulness would have a determined quality that would bring it close to pain. Papa, who would from now on spend his mornings looking for work and his afternoons patching up the house and making repairs, would be silent and withdrawn. Nothing would please him. If the girls whispered, he would speak crossly·

"What's the matter, you can't talk normal? You'd think somebody just died around here."

But if his daughters became silly as they sometimes did, he would glare at them. "*Quiet!* With you everything is funny, a joke, a big ha-ha. Go somewhere else with your ha-ha-ha. I want to think."

And so it would go until he found work again.

The girls were well trained. As they walked in the kitchen and found their father at home at four o'clock in the afternoon, lying on his back under the stove and looking up into the oven, they acted as if it were the most natural thing in the world. Tools and stove parts were spread out on a newspaper beside him.

"Can't find anything wrong with the stove, Rachel," he said to his wife. "It's worn as the very devil and could stand a good cleaning. Becky, get me a clean rag."

Becky hurried to find the rag while Mama stood at the ironing board pressing a shirt. When Papa was out of work, one of the first things Mama did was to see that all his shirts were clean and pressed, his pants brushed and cleaned, and his socks in order and mended. She did this other times as well, but not with such a fierce determination as now. Papa must look as though he respected himself when he went to find work and even when he stayed at home.

"There probably isn't anything wrong with the oven at all," Becky thought. It was only another one of Mama's devices to let Papa feel useful. Or maybe Mama saved up chores for Papa.

"Danny, that faucet is dripping in the bathtub. Do you think it needs a new washer?"

or

"Could you please help me lift the window box on the back porch? Whenever it's convenient, I mean. It's just about time to put the plants outside."

Mama could very well do these things by herself, but maybe she was right in letting Papa feel useful. Even so, Becky hated it when her father was out of work. The house felt different; everyone acted unnaturally. There was nothing to do but wait, not knowing if it would be two days, two weeks, two months, or even more. And although the Goldens had never touched bottom, Becky always thought of the long lines of unemployed people standing at the free kitchens and waiting in lines to get their cups of soup.

She knew the economics of being out of work. First they would use up what little money Papa had been able to save from his last job. Then Mama's dressmaking money, the little nest egg she had nurtured with such long hours of work, would disappear in rent and grocery bills. Becky noticed a hole in the bottom of her father's shoes as his feet stuck out from under the stove; he would put cardboard inside his shoe but the hole would remain unfixed until he had a job again.

Becky let herself drop in Papa's chair and sat sideways, both legs falling over one of the arms. "And now of all times I have to be hungry. Naturally. How rotten!"

And that too was how it always happened when Papa was out of work. Becky immediately developed a ravenous hunger. For the first few days meals would be more or less usual as though nothing were wrong. Then the cabbage rolls would be stuffed with rice instead of meat. Fresh fruits would disappear, then fresh vegetables; butter would have to last a long time; the children would get milk once a day; and nothing would be plentiful. Cabbage and potatoes would supply the bulk of lunches and dinners.

Even now Becky, who normally did not think about food at all excepting for an occasional desire for a pickle, craved a luxury. A bunch of fat black grapes or a banana split with puffs of whipped cream and almonds became visions, and if she managed to get rid of them other visions would take their place, a wedge of cheese cake or a roll covered with cream cheese and smoked salmon. She was starving already and she had just come home from school.

Her eyes wandered around the kitchen. In the glass bowl that was usually filled with fruit there remained but one orange. It might have been there three or four days without Becky's noticing it. Now she longed to sink her teeth in the orange peel and tear it off so she could bite into the luscious fruit inside.

"Becky, I'll bet you're hungry. Go ahead, take the orange, if you like," Mama said, as she ironed the collar of Papa's shirt.

She shook her head no. Papa loved oranges too. This would be the last one they would see for a while, so he should have it. She left the Morris chair to go to the bedroom to change from her school dress to pants and a shirt. While she was there, Mama and Dori had left to deliver a dress to a customer and Mimi had run out to go to a rehearsal of the Drama Club. In the meanwhile Papa had finished with the stove, washed up, and was already reading the newspaper when Becky came into the kitchen.

"You heard what Mama said," Papa was already sterner than usual. "She said for you to take the orange. So take it."

"No, Papa, it's for you."

"Becky, I'm not in the mood for nonsense. You take it. No more arguments."

Becky was as stubborn as her father. Papa was too difficult when he wasn't working. And yet watching him study the want ads, which he must have looked at before, she felt sorry for him, but not enough to give in.

"I'll take the orange only if you will sit at the table with me and share it like we used to do," she said softly. "Otherwise, no."

Unexpectedly Papa became meek. "Why not?" he said. Becky found two plates and a fruit knife. Deliberately and expertly without once cutting into the fruit or leaving the pulp behind, Papa peeled the orange in one long spiraling strip that did not break. He gave Becky the first segment and took the second one for himself. They ate the orange slowly, savoring its tart sweet flavor.

"An orange is a fine thing," Papa said. "Can you imagine if there were no oranges and you had to invent one? How would you think of such a thing that looks so beautiful and tastes so exquisite, something that's full of juices and yet so protected that it doesn't dry out. What a creation!"

"There's another big orange thing out there too," Becky said, as the setting sun, promising summer, glowed brightly through the kitchen window. "How would you like to invent that?"

"I leave the big things to God. It's only little gold things I make, when I can."

They were finishing the last segments of the orange and watching the sun slipping toward the horizon and Papa said in a confidential tone of voice, "No letters from Vienna. It's a long time since I've heard from him."

"Maybe he's all right but he can't feel free to write for a while," Becky said weakly, trying to cheer her father. He shook his head.

"You know, Becky, it's bad to be out of work, but it's good to be alive. It's a blessing, just to be alive. I am thinking of Bernard and all the others. You know what I'm saying, Becky?"

"I know," she said.

They sat quietly for a little while more and Becky thought she saw a look of tranquillity on Papa's face.

Papa was unemployed for two weeks this time, two weeks and a few days more to be exact. It was hard to believe times were hard in those days of sparkling spring weather, quivering with the promise of summer. Funds sank low and Mama was faced with dental work that could not wait, and her nest egg was again reduced to almost nothing.

Then one day that wonderful time everyone had been waiting for came when Papa walked into the kitchen, singing as he walked, his arms laden with bags of groceries. A package of meat, a loaf of bread, fruit almost spilling over the brown paper bag, and a small bunch of flowers for Mama.

"You found a job!" Mama cried.

He put down the bag of groceries, kissed her, and waltzed around the kitchen with her.

"And this time," he said, "I think the factory will last a while."

"Factory?" Mama asked. Papa had worked in small concerns before but not a factory. "What kind of factory?"

"Electronics. It's something new. They need someone who can handle small delicate parts. It's a defense plant, Rachel."

"Defense?" Mama asked. "It sounds like war, doesn't it, Danny?" A cloud passed over her face, but Papa, being so relieved kissed away her fear.

"It's for defense, Rachel," he assured her, "and it will mean dinner on the table every night for quite some time to come. How's that?"

And then Mama nodded. "Whatever God sends," she said.

While Papa had been out of work, Becky had realized that the closing date for the WONDER contest had passed and because she had apparently not won anything, she did not speak of it. She no longer dreamed of horses. But now that Papa had another job, the horse apparently felt free to return, for that very night she dreamed that the same palomino came to her, waited until she mounted him, and then took her swiftly across a moonlit plain.

She awoke knowing that foolish as the dream was, she must have a horse and nothing in all the world seemed able to change her wish and leave her in peace.

19

Looking toward Summer

"Boy, how I love summer! It's my favorite time!" Becky said dreamily. "We'll have to think of good things to do this summer."

"Oh Becky, every season is your favorite," Dori said. "Besides, summer doesn't come until June twenty-first." With that she put down a card and took up another from the pile, and instantly Becky's dreaminess vanished.

"Dori Golden, you're cheating. You took two turns; that's not fair. Put that card back."

"I certainly was *not* cheating," Dori retorted with wounded dignity, and put the card back. In the next instant Mickey, the kitten, pounced on the cards, discovering an exciting new game for himself and scattering the cards all over the back porch.

"Bad kitty! You naughty little cat! Mmmmm!" Only the words were harsh, but Becky's tone of voice might just as well have been whispering, "Good little kitty, what a darling you are!" She picked him up and buried her face in his soft gray fur. Everyone, even Mama, was spoiling the cat.

"Let me hold him, please," Dori begged and Becky gave her the little purring kitten.

Dori was recovering from a new grief and Becky was trying to help her get over it. Her little gamin friend Mickey had shown up one night with a tear-stained face and had blubbered good-bys. Please, they mustn't tell the cops, she begged, but her mother was leaving town early the next morning and she didn't know where they were going. Just away somewhere. Mickey pressed wet kisses on everyone and clung to Dori until a rasping female voice yelled up from below.

"C'mon, Mick, you been there long enough. Step on it now."

Mickey had pulled herself away from Dori, wiped her face on her sleeve, and disappeared down the back stairs.

Becky let Dori sleep with her, but she wept most of the night and could not be comforted, not even by Mickey the kitten, who curled up beside her. Long after Dori fell asleep, Becky lay awake and thought about the pattern of wishes.

Mimi's wish had come true because she had acted on it, and then it had dissolved. Dori's wish had come without her having done anything at all, and that too had now vanished. As for Becky's wish, it did not show the faintest sign now of ever being fulfilled.

And oh how she wanted a horse! To stroke its long soft nose and talk with it, to look into the soft moist eyes and to ride it through the fields and woods far from Hope Street. The wish burned deep within her, harder and stronger than ever.

Three days later the girls were playing cards in what they called The Summer Place, which to them was almost like The Summer Palace. In winter it was an ordinary back porch where Mama stood when she hung out the washing on the line. It commanded a view of all the other back porches in the block and the yards beneath.

One summer Mama had put a narrow mattress on the

porch and Becky liked to lie there and read. The following summer, Mama covered the mattress with a striped bedspread and four or five pillows in bright colors. Mama's plants grew from the window boxes Papa had built and reached up on a lattice of strings to form a curtain of green leaves and small pink blossoms. Three wire baskets hung from the ceiling and from these leafy plants trailed over the edges. Becky thought of the porch as her own Hanging Gardens of Babylon.

On this warm day, promising an early summer, a flock of pigeons—or were they doves—wheeled up in the sky, circled near the porch and flew off again.

"Funny, I never saw those before," Becky said.

"I've seen hundreds of pigeons," Dori said scornfully.

"Yes, but those aren't wild. I think this is someone's flock. Look, they're coming back."

They came so close that Becky could hear the whir of their wings.

"It must be nice to have birds. It wouldn't be so hard to have them here," she said dreamily, as they wheeled away.

Dori was more interested in the neighbors. The fine weather had drawn most of them outdoors.

"Look, there's Mr. Davidson, out in his garden in his undershirt. It's such a nice garden but he keeps fences around it, as if anyone would want to steal his peas and lettuce and flowers."

"He's right. They would, and they have, lots of times!" Becky said. "Look at Mr. Angelo's hound on the shed roof. That silly dog. When the moon gets high, he'll bark his silly head off all night, I'll bet."

From the next house there suddenly rose the sounds of their neighbor, Mrs. Spinelli, as she sang. It ceased for a moment and then began again as she stepped on her porch to hang up a row of baby clothes and diapers. She called out a bright hello to the girls and resumed her aria.

The girls sat quietly, listening to the sounds of the late afternoon. Someone was calling a child. Elsewhere a man and woman fought loudly. The Marcus sisters who lived nearby were setting out chairs on the porch while their radio played loudly.

"They're so nice though," Dori said. "Even if they're old and fat, they always give us cookies."

"Hope Street isn't bad," Becky said. "It's sort of human, I guess."

The flock of pigeons wheeled by once more and again the girls could hear the beating of their wings.

"If only I could fly," Dori said, dreaming.

"You'd fly to Mickey's," Becky finished her thought. "Better not think too much about what you can't have." But this warning was meant for herself as well as Dori. Forget the horse.

The first evening star appeared and Becky came close to saying "Star light, star bright . . . ," but thought better of it and said nothing.

"Let's play another game of Fish, Dori."

But the pigeons flew in a vast circle once more, the sun throwing glints of light on their wings, and the girls watched in silence.

20

Communications

"Mama, are you home?"

"Yes, Becky. Don't shout from downstairs. I'm busy now."

That meant that Mama was with a customer. These days she was so busy that she hadn't even picked up the mail. Becky expected nothing anymore for herself, but she picked up what the postman had dropped through the slot, a bill for Papa, a letter from a magazine asking for subscriptions, and finally a thin airmail letter with fine spidery handwriting. Becky pondered the handwriting as she walked up the stairs. It reminded her of Bernard's, but it wasn't his, and the stamps came from Switzerland. Did her father know anyone in Switzerland? She thought not, and put the mail behind the sugar bowl where Papa would find it when he came home.

The kitchen was clean and quiet, and bathed in the afternoon sun. Mama and her customer, who was trying on a dress, talked in low tones in the other room. Becky found crackers and a glass of milk and settled herself on the Summer Place bed with a library book. But after ten minutes of tranquillity, she closed it.

"Stupid book," she said with more vehemence than it deserved.

Miss Mould, the librarian, was particularly fond of Becky

because she was one of the most avid readers, and so she went to great pains to find books for her, many of which were splendid. *The Care and Feeding of Horses, Preparing for the Horse Show, An Encyclopedia of Horses,* and the *Best Loved Horses in History*—all these Becky had studied as though they were texts. And up to this time she had devoured any fiction, good or bad, provided it concerned horses.

"But this is a silly stupid book," she told herself. The book was about three girls who lived in a Scottish castle and rode horses every day, while becoming enmeshed in a ridiculous mystery. Miss Mould also found books for Becky about girls at French boarding schools or beautiful southern belles whose fathers bred race horses.

"I might have liked them last year," Becky grumbled to herself. "All those *wonderful* girls with their *marvelous* horses. Rotten snobs! As if I wanted to have anything to do with them!"

Her horse was only a dream. Give it up, Becky. Forget it. It's not for you. The common-sense voice spoke all too clearly.

She laid herself out on the mattress and looked idly at the tops of trees and the sky. A flapping of wings announced the flock of pigeons circling around once more. She wished she were a bird. How remarkable it would be to fly so high and not be afraid of falling!

The doorbell rang. Let it ring, she thought, because I just don't care any more.

"Becky, will you go down and see who it is, please? I'm busy." Mama spoke through a mouthful of pins and Becky answered with a sigh. Wiping the crumbs from her mouth, she got up, walked through the house and down the front stairs to see who it was.

A boy in uniform stood at the door, a telegram in his hand.

"Rebecca Golden?" he asked, holding out the envelope.

"Yes, that's me," she said breathlessly. A telegram for her? Mama was afraid of telegrams because they could carry bad news. She said good news usually came more slowly, in letters.

"Sign here," the boy said and Becky signed. He gave her the telegram and left. Becky opened the yellow envelope with trembling fingers and read it.

REBECCA GOLDEN

CONGRATULATIONS STOP YOU HAVE WON WONDER OR CASH PRIZE TWO HUNDRED FIFTY DOLLARS STOP DETAILS WILL FOLLOW

ROBERT HUNT, MANAGER

Her mouth dropped open and she could not catch her breath. The next minute she was bounding up the stairs three at a time and she burst into the bedroom, not caring if Mrs. Sach was dressed or not. She waved the telegram in Mama's face.

"I won, Mama! I won! I'm getting a horse, a live horse! WONDER! See, Mama, I did it, I won!"

Tears ran down her cheeks and she began to laugh. Without the slightest doubt, she was the happiest girl possible in all the world.

21

A Celebrity

Within fifteen minutes the life of the Golden family was magically changed. How the news spread so quickly was a mystery Becky did not have time to think about. The telephone rang constantly as newspaper reporters called. A feed and grain firm wanted Becky to use their products for her horse. A woman's page reporter wanted a special interview and three reporters and two photographers from rival newspapers were already sitting in the living room, pencils in hand, asking questions.

Mama could not imagine where all the children came from, but more than a dozen stood on the front porch and begged to see the horse. Mama, beside herself with confusion, had to promise them they could see the horse as soon as it came.

Upstairs the reporters quizzed Becky.

"Were you surprised when you learned that you won?"

"What did you say on the contest blank?"

"Are you going to keep him, Becky? Where?"

The reporters seemed to shoot these questions at her, one after the other, and Becky, balancing on the arm of a chair answered with a shrug of her shoulders, a giggle, or a half sentence that did not say much. Everything was happening too fast.

"Let's have a nice smile now. For the front page!"

"We'll take more pictures of you when the horse comes."

"Do you know how to ride, Becky?"

"And what do you think of all this, Mrs. Golden?"

Poor Mama was flustered at this invasion of her calm quiet world. She was afraid of what reporters would write, and her most frequent word was "please" which really meant "leave us alone."

When the doorbell rang again, Mimi went down and let in Mr. Howell, the local company representative of Bixies. Immediately sizing up the situation, he brought the interviews to a rapid finish with long-practiced tact and promised more interviews later. Mama offered him a chair and expressed her gratefulness once the reporters had left.

"Well, I guess this is a surprise, even a shock, to all of you," he said. "Becky, we do have matters to discuss and that's why I sent the reporters away. I'm glad you didn't talk too much. First of all, you know, don't you, that you don't have to take the horse. You can have the money instead."

"But I want the horse, Mr. Howell. All my life I've wanted a horse!" Becky assured him.

"Yes, of course you do. But there are problems. For one thing, where will you keep the horse? He will need a stable and there must be a guaranty that he will be cared for and fed. One of the grain companies will help you out for a while for the publicity, but eventually it will be your responsibility to house and feed him. The SPCA can make it very uncomfortable for you if you don't have adequate shelter for him."

Becky looked around the room helplessly. "I hadn't quite thought of it."

The vision of the Happy Horse Stables crossed her mind. Perhaps she could find some way to keep WONDER there. Then she would be like the elegant girls she had seen there that day when she went to look for work. But she could not think straight. The confusion in the house was too much, the telephone ringing and the endless stream of children, most of whom she did not know, knocking at the door and wanting to see the horse.

Mr. Howell was sympathetic. "I can see this is a problem and you haven't had time to think it over, but I'll see if I can locate a stable for you. I've seen WONDER and he really is just that, a handsome horse. Well, Becky, don't talk to any reporters but think it over carefully and I'll be back in two days. Remember, it's no disgrace to take the money. Here's my card, Becky, and call me if you want to talk it over some more."

Becky thanked him. "But I know there'll be some way to keep WONDER."

"You have a lovely daughter, Mrs. Golden. Becky, my congratulations!"

Mama and Becky went to the door with Mr. Howell. Outside the children still clustered in the yard and would not go away.

"Hey, Becky, when ya gonna get the horse?"

"Hey, Becky, kin I have a ride?"

"Me, too. I'm your best frien', Becky."

Becky shut the door. The telephone was ringing upstairs.

"Too much is happening, Mama. It's like a dream. I can't believe it."

Papa heard the news on his way home. "So you got your horse after all. Bless you, Becky, what a surprise, eh?"

Somehow Mimi and Mama managed to get dinner ready, but although Becky sat at the table, she could not swallow anything. It was then she realized that Mama was far from happy about the whole matter.

"I wish you had won the tennis racquet instead. It's nice for girls to play tennis. I could make you a tennis dress, white, with pleats in front."

"Oh Mama. Anyway, I've got a tennis racquet," Becky said with disgust.

"Horses are for people who live on farms, not for city girls. You could fall and God forbid, break your neck."

"Not everybody who rides a horse breaks a neck," Papa said coming to Becky's aid. "Besides, I think Becky would be a beautiful rider. If you want to sew for Becky, you could make her riding clothes."

"Clothes I can make, but broken bones I can't mend," Mrs. Golden said, still fearful for her daughter actually in danger of riding such a beast. "Something else, too, where would you keep the horse, what would you feed him? Have you thought about that?"

"I know, Mama. I'll let *you* ride WONDER. Then you'll see how nice he is. And we'll find a way to keep him. I can work."

Mrs. Golden burst into unexpected laughter. "Me? I've never been on a horse in my life. You think I'm going to begin *now?*"

Mama's laughter was a good sign. It meant that sooner or later she would get used to the idea and accept WONDER. In honor of Becky's good fortune, Mimi offered to take her turn at the dishes, and Becky, too restless to stay at home, flew off to see Lisa Kline.

22
The Wind Shifts

Lisa threw her arms around Becky as soon as she saw her. "I am so *happy* for you! I wanted to go over and see you, but there were so many kids milling around your yard. Of course I would die if *I* won a horse. I wouldn't know what to do with it. But I know, Becky, it's just what you wanted!"

Lisa led Becky into her pink and white bedroom and the girls sat on the bed. "It's true, Lisa, I'm so happy. Pinch my arm, tell me I'm not dreaming."

"Of course you're not. Have you seen the evening paper yet? Wait a minute." She returned from the kitchen with the clipping already cut out for her scrapbook. "See, GIRL WINS HORSE, and there you are!"

Becky giggled and turned red to see a picture of herself looking somewhat giddy and her eyes wide open, as if she had been saying "Who? Me?" How embarrassing it was and yet how intoxicating to find herself looking at her from the newspaper!

At nine o'clock she drifted home. For five hours now she knew she had won a horse but she still could hardly believe it.

As she climbed the back stairs she was aware of an uncomfortable feeling, nothing she could define, only a suspicion that something was wrong. She was sure of it when she saw the family sitting around the bare kitchen table. Dori was leaning against Mama; Mimi was biting her fingernail, then stopping, then starting again and that showed she was upset; but Papa was the focus as he sat rigidly looking at nothing, his eyes like burning coals. In front of him on the table, thin airmail sheets of paper lay spread out.

"What's the matter? What's happened?" Becky asked.

They all spoke at once. "Come sit down," Mama said.

"Cousin Bernard—a letter from Switzerland."

"Little David might come and be our baby brother," Dori piped up.

Then Becky remembered. "That's right, a letter came from Switzerland. I forgot to tell you."

"It slipped to the floor and I found it when we were sweeping up after dinner," Mama explained.

"Bernard has pneumonia!" Dori exclaimed, eyes wide with horror. "He's real sick."

"First he had to get out of Vienna," Mimi interjected.

"Please, will someone begin from the beginning," Becky begged, sitting down by her father.

"Yes, I think I'd better tell her." Becky was shocked at his voice; it was his most solemn way of speaking. "I'll translate the letter for you." He began to read and everyone listened as intensely as they must have listened the first time.

Dear Dan:

I cannot say much and a kind nurse is doing the actual writing because I am very ill. Pneumonia. What has happened sounds too much like an adventure story to be real, but it is real enough.

As you may know . . . I'm not sure how much information has reached you . . . events have been grim beyond

description for those of us in Vienna. For a
while I was somewhat protected by an official who
wanted me spared, but his influence was short-lived.

One night while I was performing with the symphony . . .

Here Papa broke off as the telephone rang. "I'll get it. It
may be Mr. Freeman!" he cried as he went to answer it.

"Mama, what is this all about?" Becky asked.

"I'll tell you briefly and later Papa will translate the
letter. Someone warned Bernard that the secret police were
going to arrest him sometime during the night. He managed
to get home and take Anna and David with him to the house
of a friend where they hid. Then, disguised in country
clothes so that they looked like farmers, the three of them
made their way to Switzerland, all across Austria. Friends
helped all along the way. First they were hidden under a
tarpaulin in a truck; once they spent two days in a barn. But
they managed. It was very cold even this late in the year,
and they were clearly visible against the snow.

"When they got close to the Swiss border, they were
advised to separate. Bernard carried David, and Anna went
alone. But just as she reached the border, the guards
discovered her and shot her. She may have died right away.
Bernard wanted to go to her, but it was more important to
save David, and he was able to cross the border. Someone
picked him up and took him to a place outside of Zurich,
and there he was put in a hospital. When he came to, he
was told that Anna was dead but that David was all right.

"Well, he is very sick. In this letter he asks us to take care
of David here until he gets well enough to come and join his
little boy."

"We're going to do it, aren't we?" Becky asked.

"No question about it. Of course. The only problem is it
takes money to get David over here. Bernard had to leave

everything behind, even his violin, so he has nothing. If we can raise the fare for David to come, an organization will take care of getting him here to us."

"But we don't have the money," Mimi said. "Papa's trying to borrow some."

Papa had finished his telephone conversation. "I'm going to talk with Freeman now. I'll be back as soon as I can," he said as he walked out.

Mama explained. "You see, Mr. Freeman is the head of a committee that takes care of refugees. The committee had money, but it had to help so many people there's almost none left. And when Papa was out of work—even though it was for such a short time—it took our savings. So we're trying to borrow. I'm sure we will, one way or another."

The thought passed Becky's mind that she could give them the money outright. But then what would happen to WONDER?

"Could Uncle Charlie lend Papa the money?" she asked her mother.

"For one thing Uncle Charlie is in Chicago so we can't talk with him. But anyway, Papa knows and I know that his money is all tied up right now and he can't get to it. A month from now, maybe yes, but now? The money just isn't there."

"And I think about that poor little boy without his mother and his father sick. It must be awfully hard on him."

"I'm sure that's the truth. Poor little darling! But we'll make it up to him once he gets here. And then Bernard will get well and when Bernard comes here, what a happy day that will be!" Mama said. Then she looked at the clock. "How late it's getting and tomorrow you have school. So best for you to get some sleep. Here let me kiss you goodnight. What good girls you are, all three of you!"

She's already forgotten about my horse, Becky thought,

but she kissed her mother goodnight. The air of sadness spread through the house.

Mimi fell asleep immediately, but Becky tossed restlessly. Why must everything happen at once, she demanded of nobody. Why couldn't she have won her horse two weeks earlier or two weeks later when there would be no possibility of issues being confused. Or why couldn't Bernard and his family have tried their escape some other time, either much earlier or at least a week later. Well, she was going to get her horse anyway and Papa would surely find the money somewhere.

She tried to picture herself sitting on Wonder, riding him from the Happy Horse Stables to the woods beyond while everyone admired her horsemanship. But as she fell asleep, her dream was full of fevers and Victoria Park turned into Austria with nightmare views of Bernard hiding in the snowy woods at night, or a small boy speechless with fear, and the lovely Anna fleeing across the field to the border, only to fall as the shot rang out and the bullet pierced her heart. Becky could see the blood staining the snow and the police who had shot her looking down at the fair young woman to make sure she was really dead.

Becky turned restlessly in her sleep and tried—literally made herself—recall the picture of Wonder that had appeared on the box, the beautiful horse with the black mane. She longed for him to appear and to take her away but he did not come. As she fell asleep again she thought that the photograph Aunt Martha had given her of her father and Bernard had come alive and the two boys with the haunting eyes were talking with one another. The kitchen door opening woke her up. It might have been eleven o'clock or later. She tiptoed to the door and listened and watched.

"Any luck, Dan?" her mother asked. This was not a

dream. It was real and Becky listened intently.

"Not a bit. The committee's funds have been drained dry. Freeman and I signed all the papers and everything is in order. David can come as soon as we can pay for him. But Rachel, where am I going to borrow the money? Banks are difficult because there are too many cases like these. It's not exactly business for them, not what they call an investment."

"Can't Freeman help?"

"He will try, he says, and I believe him. He's a good man. But even he says it's not easy, and he's a very persuasive man."

"Maybe he'll find it. One way or another, Dan, we're going to get that child over here. If only my customers were rich. . . . But then, if they were rich, they wouldn't be coming to me."

Becky standing in the doorway, saw Papa put his arm around his wife. "It's no question, Rachel. One way or another we'll find a way to get David. And we should write to Bernard immediately and let him know. Whoever would have dreamed things would work out this way? How could anyone tell?"

It was the same question Becky had been asking herself. She slipped back into bed and fell into a dreamless sleep. It was all too much and she could not think about it any more, not for a single minute.

23

A Decision

Never had a day been more difficult for Becky. She felt as if she had not slept for a week and going to school was a torture instead of the victory she had once imagined. Everybody clustered around her, friends and new-found friends, asking the same endless questions.

"How did you ever do it, Becky?"

"When is your horse going to come?"

"If it's a girl horse and if it has a colt, can I have it?"

Becky pretended to grin and shook her head. "Look, I haven't even seen the horse yet. I don't want to talk about it. See?"

It was easier to sit in a class, for when she was asked how it felt to be a winner and when notes asking if she would let her good friend Charlie (or Louise or Sam or Don) ride Wonder, all she had to do was nod and withdraw to her own thoughts.

"I must hold on to myself," she thought, "and think only about school, and when I go home afterward, Papa will have found the money somewhere." She forced herself to concentrate on history and math, but at the edge of her mind she caught glimpses of a horse running wild and when she blinked it away, she saw a small frightened boy looking at her, a very young boy with large eyes, like hers.

"I hate money," she cried to herself in a silent outburst.

Why did the company offer a choice, *WONDER* or money? Money was only green paper and round pieces of silver and copper. But it could buy a horse. It could buy a house for Mama. It could save the life of a little boy.

"Well, for a girl who has just won a magnificent prize, you seem very calm," Miss Robertson said pleasantly. "You're quite a heroine, winning such a fine horse. Won't you stand up and tell us how you entered the contest and what your entry was like? And when will you get your horse?"

Miss Robertson smiled at her encouragingly, not able to understand why Becky suddenly seemed so withdrawn. Probably not enough sleep with all the excitement, she reasoned.

Blushing poppy-red, Becky managed to get to her feet. "It isn't anything very much. I sent in two boxtops of Bixies and wrote in 25 words why I liked them. That's all. Nothing is really settled," she finished, mumbling, and sat down again.

"I guess we have a very modest girl with us today. But you keep us up-to-date on it, won't you, Becky?"

Becky's cheeks blazed all over again and when school was over, she escaped all her new friends who wanted to talk with her and ran home. If Papa had found the loan, then she would really let herself think about Wonder, and not a minute sooner.

She found the answer all too soon. Papa was home all right, pacing up and down the kitchen and looking furious. Mother sat at the table hemming a dress and Aunt Clara sat beside her.

"Papa, didn't you get the loan?" Becky cried and Mama hastily put her finger to her lip, meaning she shouldn't bother her father.

"There's money for everyone and everything in the

world," Papa said, "but not even a little bit to save a small boy."

"Did Mr. Freeman try everything?" she asked, having a hard time keeping her voice from shaking.

"Yes, he did, Becky. I was there. I heard him. He called ever so many people. But who's got money?"

"I do," Becky thought.

"Becky, let me give you a cup of tea. You look so pale, darling. And it was such a big day for you yesterday and we haven't even talked about it," her mother said.

Becky sat at the table and let her mother give her a cup of tea. She drank in the hot fragrant liquid and felt herself grow calm. Here she was in this warm familiar kitchen where nobody had to be afraid. It was a small world where people were warm and loving. There would be room for a homeless little boy. She felt the gold locket, touching it as though it held a secret.

Then she went to the telephone. Mr. Howell's card was lying beside it. She dialed his number, spoke to one secretary, then another, and finally heard Mr. Howell himself.

"Hello there, Becky, our first prize winner. How are you today?"

"I'm fine, Mr. Howell, and how are you?"

"I'm fine too. What can I do for you, Becky?"

She tried to keep her voice from shaking. "Mr. Howell, I've been thinking about the horse and what you said about how hard it is to keep it, and I guess there isn't any place on Hope Street, and. . . ."

"Well, you're a sensible girl, Becky. Are you saying you'd rather have the money? It's a wise choice. You can do so much with money and I tell you, a horse can be a bother. My daughter had one and I know. At first it's a novelty and then it's a burden."

As he talked, praising Becky for her wise decision, tears

rolled down her cheeks. Mr. Howell asked if he could come over that evening because he would have to talk with her parents too. Becky washed her face, took a deep breath to get herself back in control, and then went back to the kitchen.

"Papa," she said. "I guess you'd better call Mr. Freeman and tell him you've got your loan. And after tonight he'll be able to get everything started so that David can come over and be with us."

Her father looked at her. "What on earth are you talking about?"

"Don't ask me any more now. Just tell Mr. Freeman to come over later on tonight." And she ran into her bedroom, because her voice was shaking, tears were threatening, and she was afraid her father would talk her out of her decision.

It was a long argumentative evening with Papa refusing to accept money from his daughter and Becky, now cool and decided, insisting that if he did not take the check Mr. Howell had brought over to her personally, she might as well tear it up, for she had no further use for it. Fortunately Mr. Freeman interrupted, for with these two hotheads, he later explained, anything might have happened. He finally calmed Papa down and explained that if he did not accept Becky's offer, most likely he would not find any money at all anywhere. And time was of the greatest importance. That little boy needed help now.

"All right," Papa said at last, and then he took Becky's head between his two hands and kissed her. "What a person you are, Becky!"

But he said he would not accept the money until Mr. Freeman drew up a note saying that Papa would repay Becky every cent he borrowed within a certain amount of time and interest besides.

"It must be a legal transaction," he insisted. "I don't take money from my children. Not ever."

"Please, Papa, I don't care. Money is meant to be used and it doesn't matter to me." Becky had a throbbing headache by this time and wished everyone would go home. Then in the privacy of her bedroom, she could weep and grieve for Wonder.

At last Mr. Freeman left and she went to bed. Lying safely under the covers, Becky's eyes were wide in the darkness and she did not weep after all. Everything was solved, everything was clear.

"I'll never have a horse now," she said to herself and knew it was the truth. Papa would pay back the money, there was no doubt about that, but she knew that she would never be able to buy a horse. Maybe when she grew up she would have one, because then she would be free to live as she liked. But it would not be the same.

After a long time she fell asleep. In this, her last horse dream, she stood at the edge of a plain. Wonder rode up from a distance and stood before her, his long black mane gleaming in the moonlight and his proud flanks glistening. Becky patted his long nose and he looked at her with huge velvety eyes, but she did not mount him. He stepped back and bowed to her, lowering his head slowly and gracefully before her. Then he lifted it, turned, and riderless, galloped into the distance until she could see him no more.

24

Aftermath

Within two weeks Wonder was forgotten by almost everyone. Everyone that is but Becky. First there had been widespread disappointment.

"You mean you're not going to TAKE the horse, not even when you won?"

"Becky, how could you? I thought you loved horses."

"G'wan, she's scared. You talk big, Becky, but when it comes to actually getting a horse, you're yellow."

"Hey, whattcha gonna do with all the money, huh?"

Becky's attempts at a dignified silence were sometimes failures. She refused to talk about any of it although she almost shouted at one accuser.

"Of course I'm not scared, you DUMB IDIOT! Bring me a horse and I'll show you who's afraid. It's not me."

She cringed almost as much when her friends discussed it.

"Taking the money was so much more sensible. Where could she keep a horse?"

"Yeah, and it's a western horse, so it would probably be miserable in the city. Horses even get nervous breakdowns."

Would they never tire of discussing it, Becky wondered. Once she had even exploded. "Don't talk about it any more, *please!*" and then her friends stopped, surprised because Becky had always been so gentle. Among themselves they discussed the matter and could not understand Becky, and

she would not explain that the money was needed for
David, because it had hurt Papa's pride to accept the
money. The least she could do she felt was keep quiet about
it.

The talk died down, but her life had changed. There was
a void where the dream horses had romped so carefree
through dull classes or through long rainy Sunday afternoons at home. Now she had to squirm through the last days
of school like everyone else. Nor could she dream any more
of the saddle she would have for her horse or the places
where they would ride together.

Books were a solace. One afternoon, a few days before
David was to arrive, Becky was lying on the mattress of The
Summer Place, reading a new novel about a horse that Miss
Mould had ordered especially for her. "Oh how you will
love it!" Miss Mould had said.

Becky read a few chapters and then, for no reason at all,
threw the book hard across the porch. It slammed against
the railing and fell wounded on the floor.

Becky sat up, frozen with shock. "What's happening? Me,
Becky, throwing a book like some stupid monster? I love
books, even dumb ones."

She picked up the book, smoothed its pages and kissed it
on the cover in apology. She had been taught to respect
books and what she had done was, in her mind, a sin.

Books about horses were meaningless now. Her dream of
horses had vanished. It was over, all over. And the place
where the dreams had bloomed was now empty and aching.

She sat on the pillows and looked up into the empty sky.
"I'm not anywhere," she said, "not anywhere at all."

25

A New Brother

"Papa's late. It's after nine already," Mimi said.

"When will he get here?" Dori asked for the twentieth time that night.

"He'll get here when he gets here," Mama said. "You know as much as I do about it. You can't take a little child off the plane, just like that. You have to show credentials and make arrangements. It's complicated. But don't worry. He'll get here."

The small boy could not know what a major event his arrival was becoming in the lives of the Golden family. For the last two weeks they could think of little else. Mama and the girls had made over Dori's tiny room to a suitable place for a small boy and Dori moved in with her sisters. It meant that they were crowded, but Becky begged to be allowed to sleep on the porch and although Mama did not quite approve, she finally agreed. And on the day of his arrival, when Papa had borrowed Uncle Charlie's car to go to the airport and pick up David, Mama and the girls cleaned and polished the house as though there was going to be a celebration. Mimi had made a small cake with frosting and candles, even if it wasn't anyone's birthday, and Dori sewed a stuffed rag doll for David.

"Mama, so much of this work is silly. Do you suppose David will notice that you waxed the floor and cleaned the windows?"

"Of course not, Mimi. How would he know about such things?" But he will feel that we want him to be with us, poor little fellow. Besides, don't you think the house looks better?"

Mimi admitted that Mama always had the last word.

David would have not only a new home, but a new family as well. His father died and everyone was grateful that he lived long enough to know that David would be going to the Goldens and there was no question but that Papa and Mama would adopt him.

"Can he speak English?" Dori asked.

"He'll learn," Mama said. "I learned, your father learned, and with three big sisters to help him, he will learn too. But we don't need to start teaching him tonight. We must be very easy going because everything will be so new to him, the little darling."

Becky alone had nothing to say. It occurred to her that the most incredible wish of all, Papa's desire to have a son, was coming true, and she prayed that this one would turn out all right. Somehow she thought it would.

To her surprise she suffered a feeling of loss when Cousin Bernard died, for she had somehow expected him to live. In the photograph of him and her father, both boys seemed to have such vitality that she could hardly imagine one of them dead. In a way Becky felt linked to him, now that she had had so much to do with David's coming.

The telephone rang, a brisk sudden ring that made everyone jump. It was only Aunt Clara wanting to know if David had come yet.

"Pretty soon. Clara, I'll call you later. All right?"

Mama had had to tell everyone regretfully that David could have no visitors for a few days, so that he would have a chance to get used to his new home, and not be confused by too many people.

It was past Dori's bedtime and she tried not to yawn. Mimi turned the radio on softly, and at last the door downstairs opened and then Papa was walking into the living room with a little boy sitting on his shoulders. Papa put him down carefully and for a moment he stood alone, staring at everyone with large astonished eyes. Then he hid his face in Papa's coat.

"This is your new brother," Papa said, the pride shining in his eyes. Then he spoke to David in Yiddish in a soft voice: "Let's sit down together, shall we?"

Papa sat on the sofa and David climbed on his lap, burying his face in Papa's shoulder. Now and then curiosity overcame his fear and he peeked out to look at his new family, but turned back to the safety of Papa's shoulder again.

"Look," Becky said, "he looks just like us! He really *could* be our little brother."

The fact had struck them all that like his own father and like Papa and like the three girls, David had the same surprising blue eyes, the sooty look of the long lashes and the thick black curly hair. Although all of them were thin, David seemed particularly frail and the dark circles under his eyes touched them all.

"I wish we could make him feel at home," Mama said. She had most winningly invited him to come to her, but he had only clung to Papa all the harder, which made Papa happy enough.

Dori gave him the little doll she had made, but he let it fall to the floor. Mimi offered him a cookie, and then a tiny cup of hot chocolate, but he shook his head no. Mama assured the girls that this was hardly personal; they had to expect David to feel strange.

Mickey, now a half-grown cat with soft gray fur, rubbed against Becky's leg. Becky picked him up, stroked him until he purred and then, kneeling beside Papa, put Mickey on his lap.

"Kitty, nice kitty, pretty kitty!" she said softly as she stroked the kitten.

David peeked out from the safety of Papa's shoulder, more curious than afraid, but still shy.

"What a nice kitty, nice, nice kitty!" Becky repeated in a soothing voice.

The ghost of a smile appeared on David's face as he bent forward to stroke Mickey. Becky prayed for Mickey's cooperation.

"Nice kitty, nice, nice kitty!" David repeated, imitating Becky's inflection exactly.

And a "nice kitty" Mickey was indeed, not even defending himself when David almost put a tiny finger in Mickey's golden eyes. Moving carefully, Becky put Mickey on David's lap and let him hold the kitten. After the courtesy of a poised minute, Mickey jumped down and walked into the dining room. Fear forgotten, David slid down from Papa's lap to follow Mickey. Then, remembering that he was in a strange house, he stopped short with a new attack of shyness.

But the ice was broken and the fear was gone. Though David still clung to Papa, he was soon engaged in a game of Peek-a-boo with Mama, and one by one he regarded each of his new sisters.

Mimi offered him the little cup of chocolate again, and this time he drank it. He yawned. Without hesitation, he went to Mama and let her bathe him and dress him in the new pajamas she had made for him. Dori gave him the doll once more and this time he clutched it. Within minutes he was fast asleep in his new bed.

26

The End of a Wish

Summer was one lemon yellow day following another, and this one promised to be like other summers with birds chirping early in the morning, pitchers of lemonade in the slow lazy afternoons and long walks with Lisa. But these early summer days, pleasant as they were, would soon be over, for Lisa had been invited to spend the summer at the beach with an aunt.

"I'll miss you," Becky said and she meant it.

Even though it was Lisa who did most of the talking and Becky the listening, and even though Lisa did not always understand Becky, still they were friends, and they had always spent summers together. Becky would miss her indeed.

"But you'll find someone else or something else to do," Lisa said. "Really, Becky, you should."

For even Lisa understood that Becky felt curiously empty these days.

No summer had ever been like this one. A little brother made all the difference. At first everyone had to be particularly careful to be gentle because David was delicate and nightmares woke him up screaming sometimes as much as three times in one night. Nor did it make it easier that he did not understand English. Mama and Papa could talk with him but the girls spoke to him in English.

Then, almost within the first week, he began to look better. The nightmares appeared less often, the dark circles under his eyes vanished. The girls were able to relax with him and they took delight in teaching him to speak. Sometimes Dori dressed him almost as though he were one of her dolls, and like a little boy, he stood for this only so long, and then demanded that she play ball with him.

Mimi taught him rhymes and applauded extravagantly when he repeated them to her in what she thought was the dearest little accent she had ever heard.

But it was Becky that he loved. Ever since that first night when she had shown him the cat, he had looked at her and trusted her. After he learned to say "Papa," he said "Becky," and followed her everywhere. And so she had little choice but to take him to the library with her when she went and find books for him, or let him walk beside her when she went to the grocery for her mother. She was proud of him, and yet, he was becoming very much the little brother, always wanting to follow her.

Sometimes, such as this evening at dusk, when she sat in Papa's chair and looked out ahead and saw nothing in particular, he would climb into her lap and demand that she play horsey. And so she held him on her knee and bounced him up and down.

> Ride a cockhorse
> to Banbury Cross.
> See a fine lady
> upon a white horse.

David tried to repeat the words and became hopelessly mixed up. Becky began to laugh, for he was such a darling little fellow; then she held him in her arms, hugged and kissed him until he laughed and called out "Shtop, Becky, shtop, shtop!"

"Wait," she said, "I've got something for you, David."

She went into her room and came out with her baseball cap. She put it on his head and immediately it slipped down over his ears and eyes, for it was much too big. But he was ecstatic. Becky held him up to the mirror so he could admire himself in this big boy's cap.

Suddenly he threw his arms around Becky and kissed her with a wet child's kiss. Becky smiled as she wiped her face. It was nice to have a little brother after all.

The caressing warmth of June gave way to the fevered orange days of July. Heat shimmered upward from the pavements and the streets. In the heat of the afternoon, the streets were almost deserted.

One afternoon while David napped and the whir of Mama's sewing machine floated through the summer heat, Becky sat alone on the porch and tried to read. But she had been reading too much lately and she wanted something more than books. Mimi seemed to be away much of the time as she found baby sitting jobs and Dori had a new friend on the next block. Lisa had gone to the beach and Becky was alone much of the time. The leaves of Mama's plants that climbed and curled on their trellises cast green reflections across the porch and cooled the heat of the pale blue summer sky.

Even in the heat of the afternoon, the white pigeons came flying in a wide arc, their wings fluttering white against the sky; they turned to fly the other way and disappeared as rapidly as they had come. How lovely they were! They must be very special birds, perhaps racing pigeons or doves, Becky thought, for they were somehow different from street birds.

"I wonder what it would be like to raise a flock," Becky thought. "I should love to hold one and to feel its softness. And then it would be nice to see the babies come out of their shells. And how fine it would be to see them fly away and to know they would return."

Something about the birds had been tugging at her mind since she had first seen them. Once or twice it had occurred to her that it might be possible to raise them. It should not be too difficult to build a shelter for them in the backyard. Yet she did not yet feel free enough to go ahead.

Getting up she went into the kitchen. Her upper lip was covered with perspiration and she knew the kitchen with its electric fan was cooler than the outdoors, yet she longed to get away. As she sat on a kitchen chair, her mother spoke to her.

"I thought you were reading. Wasn't it a good book?"

"Oh Mama, I can read only so much."

"What about sewing? Do you want to finish those shorts you began?"

Becky sighed. "Let's face it, Mama. I just don't like sewing. I hate to disappoint you, but that's how it is."

"Don't worry. I'll finish the shorts and I'm not that disappointed. Some of us are made for one thing and some for another."

Becky wondered vaguely what her purpose was, and she couldn't find any. Just then a sleepy David, waking from his nap, wandered into the kitchen wearing only a pair of trunks. Mama was so busy on a fussy georgette evening gown, that Becky picked up her little brother and held him on her lap. She touched his curly dark hair with her cheek. How soft he was and how sweet. Suddenly she wanted to do something for him.

"Davy, let's go to Victoria Park together and if Mama has some dry bread, maybe we can feed the ducks. Would you like that?"

"Ducks! Ducks! Feed ducks!" David was now fully awake and would have left the house in nothing more than his little trunks.

Mama loved the idea and said if only she didn't have to finish the dress, she too would have liked going. She insisted on giving Becky bus fare and something more for ice cream cones. "You are a good daughter, Becky, and a good sister too!"

And so it was not even an hour later that Becky and David were walking over the wide green lawns of the park down to the pond where the ducks were resting idly under the willow trees or drifting on the still waters. As David threw a crust on the water, two spotless white ducks swam over to snatch them; half a dozen assorted mallards joined them and soon ducks were coming from all over the pond. Sweetest of all was a brown mother duck with her brood of ducklings who came to find out what was going on. David, intoxicated with his popularity, spoke to the ducks in several languages as he fed them and they answered him in one language, an appreciative and at the same time demanding quack.

It was then on an impulse that Becky looked up and saw beyond the farther shore of the pond the figure of a girl riding a white horse along the bridle path that stretched out from one pine woods to another. The heat shimmered and it might have been a mirage, so slowly did the horse seem to move, yet the girl and the horse were real enough. Soon they disappeared from view.

"It is very beautiful, that girl and that horse," Becky said, and then there seemed to be a great burst of light within her. She had been able to see a girl on a horse without longing to take her place and without suffering the agony of wishing. Now that she knew that, she felt a freedom such as she had not known for a long time, and she breathed a sigh that meant she had arrived at peace at last. For a while at any rate.

David had come to the last of his crusts and crumbs and now with a shout and one extravagant gesture, he threw them all into the water at once. He laughed and then turned to look up at Becky as the ducks scrambled and quacked complainingly and dove for whatever treasures they could find.

How alive he was, this little brother of hers and how close he had come to not being alive at all. Becky remembered the words her father had quoted to her so many times and now they made more sense than ever before. "Just to be alive is a blessing. Just to live is holy!"

Then she swept David up in her arms and hugged him, and though he did not understand why she was laughing, he was ready to join her and he laughed too.